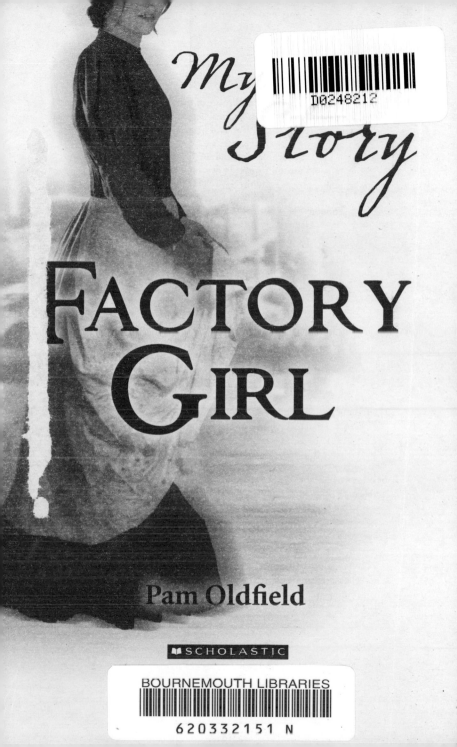

My Story

FACTORY GIRL

Pam Oldfield

■SCHOLASTIC

While the events described and some of the characters in this book may be based on actual historical events and real people, Florence Finch is a fictional character, created by the author, and her diary is a work of fiction.

Scholastic Children's Books
Euston House, 24 Eversholt Street,
London, NW1 1DB, UK
A division of Scholastic Ltd
London ~ New York ~ Toronto ~ Sydney ~ Auckland
Mexico City ~ New Delhi ~ Hong Kong

Published by Scholastic Ltd, 2011

ISBN 978 1407 11672 3

4 6 8 10 9 7 5 3

Friday, 25th May 1888

I am sitting here in Grandpa's gloomy old room and he is sitting at the table with his head resting on his arms ... and he is quite dead. It was such a shock but I have stopped crying and will soon have to go home and tell Ma the sad news. As I look round the stuffy room (which smells of his favourite peppermints), I hope he has gone to a better place.

Grandpa was writing in his beloved diary when it happened. I was sewing a button on his other shirt when he suddenly pushed the diary across the table and said, "You carry on with this, young Flo. I'm done with it."
I never could get him to call me Florence. Florence Finch. It was always Flo or Florrie or even Flossie!. Then he folded his arms on the table and put his head on his arms. He stopped breathing and when I spoke to him he made no answer – and never will again.

So now I have his diary and, to please him, I must write my own news in it. And I can. Grandpa taught me to read and write years ago. The diary is very shabby, bound in faded red leather, and more than half of the pages have been written on by him but there are plenty of pages left for me. Grandpa reckoned I was bright. Called me "the brightest of the brood" and I dare say I am, though I don't boast about it. (Who would listen?) Ma always insists that common sense is more important than being bright and calls me "clever-clogs" when she thinks I'm getting too uppity.

Grandpa always said I took after him in the brains department. He never forgave his son for marrying Ma (so she tells us) because she came from a family of costermongers and used to sell apples from their barrow.

Grandpa inherited dozens of books from an uncle and lived off them, selling them one at a time when he needed money. You could say he died at the right time because he only had three books left.

He loved old sayings. He had one for everything. One of his favourites was "Many a true word spoken in jest" and another was "Ne'er cast a clout 'ere May be out!" Oh yes! "Ne'er sup with the devil!" As if I would! According to Grandpa, if you make a pact with the devil you would live to regret it. (A pact is an arrangement). I wouldn't dare, I told him, and he laughed.

There were four of us youngsters but now there are only three. Big sister Ellie died last year from the hateful phossy jaw (from dipping the matches at the Bryant & May match factory where she worked). There's eight-year-old

Annie (who gets called Hopalong at school because of her crooked foot) and baby Dora, who's only six months old.

And me. I'll be seventeen soon and now I'll have no need to come here to Grandpa's room to look after him. I shall go to work in the match factory like all the other girls. Emma, my friend, will be there and Kitty, Ma's best friend. I shall earn some proper money at last. Three cheers for that!

I'll go home now and tell Ma about Grandpa. It will be a shock for Pa too when he gets home from sea. He works on the *Tally Rose* as a deck hand so he's away most of the time. The ship sails to and from the London docks which is why we live in Glint Street in Bow.

Ma sometimes says Pa must have another family somewhere because he never brings home much money. She always believes the worst – she's just made that way. I think Pa probably spends his money on ale (or gambling on cards) but I can't very well say that to Ma.

We have two rooms – a kitchen with a sink, two shelves on the wall and a stove where we can heat a kettle of water, and a bedroom. If we'd had room, Grandpa would have lived with us. He was 61. Albert Samuel Finch. Now he is like one of his sayings – "Gone but not forgotten".

Saturday, 26th May

Grandpa dying yesterday sent the family into a dither. Everyone crying, (me as well, because they set me off again), so now my eyes are all red and I look a perfect fright so I hope I don't meet Alfred. He's my young man — but only for the moment because he's a bit on the gloomy side and Ma calls him MiseryGuts (but not to his face). He, at least, will enjoy the funeral, if he decides to come.

Ma's best friend, Kitty Petts went with Ma to wash the body and lay Grandpa out and the funeral will be on Monday. We can't have bells ringing or a choir because they cost money, but the organist will play a hymn for us to sing. So it will be very quiet and about eight or nine of us will come back to the house for a bite of ham and bread and a small keg of ale. The butcher let Ma put the ham on the slate until she can pay it off because he knows she will. Not like some. Kitty lent us her plates and mugs since we don't have any to spare for visitors.

It will be a bit of a squash and not very elegant. The window leaks when it rains and makes a damp patch on the wall, but Mr Caudley, the landlord, says that if he pays to have it mended, he will have to put up the rent. Ma calls him a skinflint, but not to his face, in case he turns against us and puts us out on to the street with our bits of furniture.

One day, when we have some spare money, Ma wants to buy a nice piece of curtain to hang at our kitchen window instead of the sacks. That will cheer the place up a bit. Still, mustn't grumble because we're better off than lots of people who have to sleep in doorways or under the arches. I don't know how they survive in winter.

I signed on at Bryant & May's factory this morning so I'll start on Tuesday and that means a few bob more in the kitty. At least at the factory I'll have some cheerful company of women and girls more my own age. I will also escape from the sight of our kitchen piled up with empty matchboxes waiting for their labels to be stuck on! And the smell of the sticky paste – ugh! Annie helps out with the matchboxes when she's not at school.

Everyone says the pay for the home-made matchboxes is a disgrace. Ma earns 2d for every hundred and forty -four boxes she makes but it takes her an hour! Children like Annie can only work half as fast. It's called "home" work. Ma says it should be called slave labour because you can hardly survive just on the matchboxes if you work from home. The thin sheets of wood, rather like veneer, comes ready stamped in the shape of the boxes and you have to press them out, stick on the paper label and paste it all into shape.

Old Ma Twilley, who lived next door, got so slow at making boxes because of her eyesight that she had to give up and go into the workhouse. Kitty says it's a crying shame how the poor are treated. She says that no matter how hard you try, you can't make a better life for yourself – and that's why the workers keep going on strike. Kitty hates "the bosses" and the government, and royalty. She says there's trouble brewing.

I wanted to visit Ma Twilley but when I went to the workhouse the Master there said that he doesn't encourage visitors because it upsets and embarrasses the inmates. I don't think Old Ma Twilley would mind but he said "rules are rules". He's a mean-looking man with a red face and a scrawny neck like a turkey! I made loud turkey noises as I walked away and I know he understood because he slammed the door so hard, the whole street must have heard it.

Sunday, 27th May

No time to write much. Busy for tomorrow (the funeral), scrubbing the floor and cleaning the windows. Annie whitened the step, bless her, and took great pride in her work. She also shook the mattress she shares with Ma while Pa is away. (I sleep in a corner of the passage.) Ma kept on with the matchboxes.

After much searching I have found a good place to hide Grandpa's diary (or is it mine now?), which is inside a corner of my mattress. I miss him so much. He used to make me read to him insisting that that way I would gain a feeling for words. Now he is dead I try to read a page of his diary each day. His handwriting used to be beautiful and makes me ashamed of my own hurried scrawl. Just lately, though, his hands shook so much they splattered the ink and the words are almost unreadable. He also watered down the ink to make it last longer, so the writing is very faint. Maybe I shouldn't read it. A diary is supposed to be private.

My friend Emma is coming to the funeral. She has an older brother who is a carpet-beater (he isn't very bright because he was dropped on his head as a baby). She will look good in black with her fair curls and blue eyes. She's going to wear a black shawl and her ma's black hat.

Ma wanted us to wear our best Sunday clothes but they are all at the pawnshop and we can't afford to get them back, so we'll each have a black ribbon to wear on our left arms. Grandpa won't mind.

I saw a funeral once that had black horses with black feathers on their heads and there were men walking ahead of them with black clothes and hats with black silk ribbons that trailed down, and the coffin was in a glass carriage. It must have been someone very rich or famous. Grandpa's funeral will be very simple.

Monday, 28th May

Emma was in the church when we arrived, holding a prayer book and a bunch of violets, and looking solemn. Alfred was there also, wearing a black jacket (but it was a size too small so that his wrists stuck out from the sleeves and looked rather silly). We took baby Dora, but as soon as she started to bawl Ma gave her to me to take outside. So I missed most of the service, although I heard them singing "Onward, Christian Soldiers". It sounded a bit thin. Truth to tell it was all very depressing outside – a small, cramped graveyard with sooty tombstones and lots of tall stinging nettles. I looked down into the grave which was for Grandpa. It was very shallow and I could see the lid of another coffin, which was badly cracked and looked mouldy and horrible. At least the wood hadn't been stolen for night watchmen's fires, which sometimes happens. Ma says some people will stoop to anything!

When they came out with Grandpa I gave Dora back to Ma and stood next to Alfred to remind Emma that he was my young man. Ma had bought a bunch of white daisies to put on the coffin as it was being lowered into the grave, but as it disappeared from sight Emma stepped forward and dropped the violets in. Secretly I was annoyed. He was our Grandpa, not Emma's!

Alfred whispered, "She's hogging the limelight!" and that made me feel better. I wish I had thought about violets. It should have been me.

When we got home Emma sat down next to Alfred, but he moved further along, to talk to Annie. So maybe he isn't so bad after all, and he did once say he likes my brown eyes because they are "soulful" and likes my straight brown hair better than Emma's curls.

Kitty drank too much ale and got a bit quarrelsome but she often does that. She and Ma lived next door to each other as children and have always been friends, but Ma says Kitty comes from a rough family so we have to make allowances. Her grandfather was sent to Australia for seven years but never came back (for stealing a pair of shoes), and one of her uncles was sent to the Marshalsea prison last year for robbing a church but is out again.

Tuesday, 29th May

My first day at the factory! Hurrah! The Bryant & May match factory is in Fairfield Road so I can walk it in ten minutes. Ellie had told me what it was like inside but I was still struck dumb by how big it is – as big as a church and full of echoes, but without the pews, and the large windows are not coloured. There's a smell of oil and hot metal from the machinery and it gets into your hair and clothing.

There are stairs and more stairs, and high walkways so that the foremen can look down and spy on us all the time. To divide off the different areas of work there are walls made of iron mesh so you can see through them. It feels a bit like being in a giant cage!

I work at the benches on the first floor, which in winter is warmer than the ground floor – or so I'm told. There are thousands of empty matchboxes piled up on the work benches and you think they will never all be filled and packed but somehow it happens. If you cram too many matches into a box, it can set itself on fire and that's a waste. They call them "burnts" and if the foremen see it, we can get fined.

But I have to say it's very well organized. Some of the girls work very fast and earn quite a bit of money. I'm still rather slow – all fingers and thumbs, as Grandpa would say.

There are lots of match factories in London but ours is supposed to be very modern. It seems very noisy to me with so many people rushing about, wheeling loaded trolleys and pushing handcarts. Some workers carry armfuls of boxes and some of these are special ones with fancy foreign labels.

We girls are always gossiping, grumbling about our grievances and talking about going on strike. We never have but Emma says we might. We also sing a lot of the music hall songs to make the time pass but the foremen don't like us being happy and are always watching, in case we stop working for a few seconds. Time wasting is almost a sin at Bryant & May's. If you have to blow your nose, you get shouted at and the foremen are always looking for excuses to dock some of our pay.

There are some boys doing certain jobs but it is mostly girls and women, which is lucky for the owners (Mr Bryant, the nasty one, and Mr May, who's much nicer) because if we were all men, we'd most likely be out on strike like everyone else.

They've started me off as a packer (at one shilling and nine pence for every 100 boxes I pack). I'm very clumsy but I'll soon speed up.

I came home worn to a frazzle and now I'm dog-tired (no one sits down at the factory) and my back aches, and so do my legs. Ma says as it was my first day I can go to bed a bit earlier so I'm writing this before I fall asleep. I'll write more tomorrow.

Thursday, 31st May

Didn't write in this yesterday because baby Dora needed watching so when I came home from work I kept an eye on her while I was making matchboxes with Annie, who came home from school at dinnertime and wouldn't go back. She thinks the teacher hates her so is always dreaming up excuses to stay at home. (Today it was bellyache.) She doesn't even know her two times table.

I said, "How do you spell cat, Annie?"

She said, "K A T" and added, "You're not my teacher!"

and stuck out her tongue.

"What about horse?"

"H O S."

I hoped she was doing it on purpose, to annoy me, but I don't think she was. Ma says it doesn't matter because girls don't need an education.

Ma was round at Grandpa's house with Kitty, sorting out his things. She sold his bed, rocking chair and table for one shilling and ten pence to a second-hand furniture man. She couldn't find Lanky Josh, the old clothes man, so she pawned most of Grandpa's clothes for sixpence and will never redeem them, which means she can keep the money from the pawnbroker. Now she can pay the vicar for the funeral, and the butcher for the ham and still have a little left over.

Ma gave Grandpa's overcoat to Alfred, even though it's a bit too big for him. Hopefully his ma can take it in a bit here and there, even if she just shortens the sleeves. He's not bad looking and if he smiled more, he'd look better still. I wonder what he's like at kissing.

Thursday, 7th June

Annie was crying this morning. She says Grandpa didn't want to go to Heaven and she doesn't want to either. She's at that funny age and can't understand death. I tried to explain. "Grandpa's had his turn," I told her. "Everyone gets a turn at being alive, and while you're alive you get to do things. Some things are nice and some things aren't, and then when you get old, you go to Heaven and it's very peaceful." I think she understood.

Emma and I met up in the lunch hour. Workdays we don't see each other much because she works with the dipping frames (dipping the match heads into a phosphorous mixture). She was not her usual sunny self and I finally got her to tell me what was wrong.

"I've got toothache," she said, "and I wanted to go home but the foreman said I had to see the dentist before I went and if I didn't see him, he'd dock my morning's wages. Slimy toad, that man!"

"Which one?"

"Mr Sugden. Straggly hair, bowler hat and a bit of a squint. Proper little tyrant, he is. Why should he stop my

14

money just because I've got toothache and want to go home? It's not fair."

Emma still looks pretty, even when she's annoyed. That's not fair either, I thought.

All the foremen wear bowler hats but I didn't recall one with a squint. "So?" I asked.

"So he made me go to the factory dentist. He said there was a hole in my tooth and I had to make an appointment to have the hole filled up so the phosphorous fumes wouldn't get in and make my jaw go bad." She shrugged and stared at her boots.

Now I knew she was thinking about phossy jaw. I told her to cheer up and eat her lunch but she said her tooth ached too much and she'd lost her appetite and handed her lunch to me. It was a cold boiled potato and a few crusts of bread so I ate them so as not to waste it. "Waste not, want not." That's another of Grandpa's sayings. Not that there's ever any waste in our house. Even the crumbs get eaten by the mice.

"So are you going home now?" I asked her.

"I'm supposed to be going back to have it filled but I'm not." She glared at me as though it was my fault. "Honestly, Flo, it's horrible in that dentist room. Scary. White walls, lots of light glaring down on you, metal trays and awful pincers and things. And a chair that goes up and down. Ugh!" She shuddered at the memory.

Then she jumped down from the little wall we were sitting on and ran off home without another word. Just like Emma to upset me and then disappear. Ma says that because she was born with good looks she expects everyone to do her bidding.

Sunday, 10th June

I went to church this morning early to say a prayer for Grandpa and another one for poor Emma. She came back to work on Friday but got a proper wigging from one of the foremen for missing her appointment with the dentist. Seems that Bryant & May is very proud of its dentist's room which is supposed to help the workers to not get phossy jaw. I asked God to look after Emma because she's my best friend, though I do have another friend now – the girl who works next to me at the workbench. Her name's Patty and she's 18 and has a baby but no husband. She's always laughing and says she's got her eye on Mr Stringer ,one of the few nice foremen who isn't married.

Ma's going to take us all to the park next Saturday if it stays sunny. They've got swings and things for Annie and we'll each have a fruit ice or a toffee apple but not both.

"It's a little treat from your Grandpa," Ma told us. "I put threepence by specially. I thought he'd like us to have a little treat to remember him by."

That's just like Ma. She could have bought herself a hat from the second-hand clothes man. Lots of mothers would, but not her. If I'm ever rich – which I won't be – I'll buy her a really smart hat with feathers and ribbons and everything.

Monday, 11th June

Something funny happened today when I was coming out of the factory with Emma. A young man was there with a notebook and pencil, stopping all the workers to try and ask them questions but they wouldn't stop. Too eager to get home and so was I. My head was aching from the noise – not only people talking and shouting but the machines, and the foremen bellowing orders and trolleys rattling to and fro loaded with packs of matches ready to go to the railway station which is next door to the factory.

Anyway, I was a bit grumpy with Emma so she tossed her head and stalked off, the way she does, and the young man grabbed me by the arm. He wanted to ask me about something in the newspapers.

"About the way you're treated at the factory. About the recent strikes," he told me earnestly. "Workers not being paid proper wages. The poor being exploited. You must have heard people talking about it."

"No," I said. "I've too much to do. What with work at the factory and making matchboxes at home and helping my ma with the littl'un." I jerked my arm free and walked on, (wondering if I was being exploited), but he wouldn't take no for an answer and ran alongside me.

"I just want your views…" he began.

"I don't have any views. I've got a headache and I'm tired and hungry and –"

His eyes lit up. "That's it! Being hungry can give you a headache."

I frowned. "Who says?"

"It's the truth! Listen, I'll buy you a pie. You can eat it while we talk and then your can tell me if your headache's gone."

I love pies so it was hard to refuse and I wavered. He then increased the offer to pie, mash and gravy.

"In a pie shop," he added. "Not standing at a pie stall."

So of course I said "Yes" and we were soon settled in Charlie's Pie Shop at a nice table for two with a shiny sort of tablecloth and pepper and salt in little glass pots and all around were other people eating pie and mash with gravy. It was noisy from the chatter and very hot from the cooking, and all the windows were steamed up. I felt quite grand when he gave our order.

"And we'll have some bread and butter to go with it," he told the man.

We sat back to wait for it and by this time I'd almost forgotten my headache and was ready to talk to him. When the pie came I nearly swooned – it smelled so delicious.

"So are you happy at the factory or do you think you might go on strike?" he asked. He tipped a small amount of salt on to the table and then threw it over his shoulder. That's what you do to avoid bad luck. Grandpa would have been grinning.

"Go on strike?" I replied. "Have you lost your marbles? Of course we're not going on strike." I stuffed my mouth with pie and mash. It was scrumptious, as my sister Ellie would have said. Scrumptious was one of her favourite words. "Striking is for men," I added.

He looked disappointed by my answer. "What about having your wages docked for no good reason? Is that true?"

I remembered Emma when she had toothache but it hadn't happened to me so I shook my head. In between mouthfuls of pie and mash he was writing everything down and that made me nervous.

He went on asking questions and said he worked for the

newspapers but he didn't say which ones and I wasn't really interested. He said he was going to write an article about workers who were treated badly and not paid properly. "Sweated labour", he called it. "There's so much unrest," he said. "Dockers have been on strike, so have the coal miners and the –"

I reached for the salt and sprinkled it generously over what was left of my pie and mash. I wasn't really listening because I had only just started work at the factory and I certainly did not want to stop again.

The young man said there might be "militant action" but I said, "I don't give a fig! I don't care!"

He said the strikes would bring the country to its knees and it was no more than the government deserved. There might be fighting in the streets and the government would be held to account, (whatever that means). We don't have any truck with the government in our house. Pa doesn't like the prime minister and says he wouldn't trust him farther than he could throw him! Which isn't far.

Ma doesn't like him, either, but she likes the queen. She says she can't help being posh. Ma wanted to call me Victoria but Pa said it sounded like a railway station. I wish I had been called Victoria because it's always shortened to Vicky, which is better than Flo, Florrie or Flossie.

I said, "Good luck to them, then!" meaning the strikers. I was just being awkward, if truth be told.

20

He laughed and went on scribbling in his notebook and was looking a sight too pleased with himself so I said, "I've got a diary. My Grandpa left it to me."

He looked astonished. "A diary? Can you write, then?"

"Course I can!" I said indignantly. "My grandpa taught me years ago. I write in the diary most days. Just because I'm a factory girl it doesn't mean I'm ignorant."

"Lots of them are," he replied. "No one expects women of your sort to be properly educated."

I gave him one of my looks. Ma says they would stop an elephant at 40 paces. "I can read too, so you can put that in your pipe and smoke it!"

I was wondering whether to explain that the Finches were once a bit more prosperous because Grandpa's father worked for the railway and had his own office, and always wore a white shirt and stiff white collar. Ma said he was "very well regarded". But just then he asked if I'd heard of someone called Annie Besant.

"No," I snapped, "and I don't want to so don't bend my ear about her."

He looked at my empty plate and said I could have jam roly-poly and custard if I would stay on for another ten minutes but I had to say "No" because I should have been at home making matchboxes and it wasn't fair on Ma and Annie. They would be wondering where I was.

Now, writing all this, I wonder if I'll ever see him again.

I don't even know his name and he doesn't know mine. How foolish is that?

Tonight Annie asked me if Grandpa had woken up yet so maybe she didn't understand about death after all.

Tuesday, 12th June

I had a real fright today when I got to work. I was telling Patty about the pie and mash, and she said she'd have stayed on for another half an hour to get the jam roly-poly!

"So who was this young gent with money to burn?" she asked. "I'd like to meet him!"

I said I didn't know but he said he was writing something for the newspapers. Suddenly she whispered, "'Ere comes Sugden!" and this man came up to me and said I had to go up to the office with him because the manager wanted to speak to me.

"Looks like you're in trouble, my girl!" he said. "What 'ave you been up to?"

I stared at him, frightened and trembling because I didn't think I had done anything wrong.

Patty whispered, "Don't go, Flossie. It might be a trick

to get you on your own."

And that made me more of a tremble because we all knew that some of the foremen like to pinch the girls' bottoms! If you didn't go along with it, they could make things very difficult by telling the manager lies about you so that he docked your money.

I told him I hadn't done anything wrong but he just laughed and said, "Try telling 'im that! We'd best get you up to 'is office and quick! Tidy your 'air and show some respect. Call 'im 'sir' and don't answer back or give 'im any cheek!"

I asked if it would take long because being sent for by the manager was bad enough but losing time at my bench was worse because it meant less money.

"How the 'ell do I know. Don't ask so many questions. That's the trouble with you girls. Too much mouth!" He laughed loudly.

As I still dithered he grabbed my arm and marched me past all the other girls. One of them cried, "'Ere comes old bully Sugden!" and another girl said, "Watch him, Flossie! He's got wandering 'ands!"

They all screamed with laughter and one of them poked her tongue out at him and another one blew a raspberry which made Mr Sugden cross and he tightened his grip on my arm so much that it hurt and almost brought tears to my eyes.

We went up the stairs and along the walkway, with me struggling to free my arm and him making sure I didn't. From below one of the girls shouted up, "Do us all a favour, Flossie, and push him off the walkway!" and they all burst out laughing. He went red in the face and gave me a furious look, but I wasn't going to push him. If he got killed in the fall I'd be a murderess and be hanged, and Ma would never get over it.

Mr Sugden knocked on the manager's door, opened it and almost threw me into the room. "'Ere she is, Mr Stockton! Flossie Finch."

"Thank you, Mr Sugden. You need not stay. Please close the door after you."

I'd never seen a manager before and I didn't know what to expect. A bit of a monster, I suppose, but he looked fairly normal. But smarter in his dress. He had little wire-rimmed spectacles, not much hair, a dark suit that had never seen the inside of a pawnshop, and a stiff white collar. Oh yes – and a watch on a chain across his chest!

The office was a wonderful place with large, very clean windows and a large shiny wooden desk with brass inkwells and three pens. There were big cupboards along the walls and a shiny floor – it smelled of something, maybe polish. There was a plant on one of the window sills with long, thin leaves and no flowers, and a hat stand beside the door with a nice hat on it. I'd never been in such a nice room but

I stood there in front of the desk, shaking inside.

"I've done nothing wrong ... sir!" I whispered. "I swear it! Leastways, not that I know of."

He was giving me a keen look. "It's been brought to my notice, Miss Finch, that you were seen in conversation yesterday with a journalist who has some connections with *The Link*."

"I don't know anything about it," I told him. *The Link*? What was he talking about?

He went on. "The Link is the magazine produced by the Fabian Society and they are constantly trying to stir up trouble for the government – and for people like you and me!"

I felt sick to my stomach, quite sure he was going to sack me and then Ma would be upset. I tried to recall anything the young man had said but I was so nervous, my mind was a blank. Had he said he was a journalist? Had he mentioned *The Link*?

He leaned forwards, clasping his hands on the desk. They were spotlessly clean with nice fingernails. "I have to tell you that it was most unwise of you to talk to that journalist – or any journalist writing for any newspaper. Very disloyal to Bryant & May. This firm has given you employment so that by your own efforts you can rise above poverty and make a better life for yourself. What have you to say for yourself, Miss Finch?"

So that was my crime – talking to a journalist. How was I to know that I shouldn't? My stomach started to churn something horrible and I wondered if being disloyal to Brant & May meant I would definitely lose my job.

"He bought me a pie and mash, sir," I stammered. "With gravy. I didn't know it was disloyal. I'd seen him talking to some of the other girls…"

"Young women who had the sense to refuse to talk to him!" He wrote carefully on a sheet of paper on the desk in front of him. "Journalists are not to be trusted, Miss Finch. Their aim is to stir up discontent among the workers. They hope to foster unrest so that they have something to write about. The sooner you learn that, the better it will be for all of us."

"Yes, Mr Stockton, sir. I'm sorry."

"Some of the newspapers would like nothing better than to plunge this country into revolution."

I recalled myself saying that I didn't care a fig! "I won't talk to him again, sir," I said. I felt quite wobbly at the knees but I stood up straight and looked him in the eyes.

Then he wanted to know exactly what we talked about and I couldn't remember most of it but told him the bit about the strikes and him asking me if we were happy at Bryant & May and me saying we were. Had I said we were happy?

"I should hope so!" he said, looking stern. "I should

hope that no one in this factory would consider strike action."

Would we, I wondered? We have plenty to complain about – the long hours, dreary working conditions, fines given by spiteful foremen. Low pay? I truly didn't know about that but suppose it was low pay. Would we go on strike? Should we go on strike? I knew one thing – I'd strike if the rest did, no matter what the Mr Stockton said. It all sounded rather exciting and if we could make our lives easier by striking, and then earning more money…

Mr Stockton interrupted my thoughts. "Did you tell him about the dentist we have here for you to protect your health? That's up-to-date medical care, Miss Finch. Did you tell him about the good wages we pay our workers?"

"Are they good? I mean, I didn't know they were."

He looked thunderous at that but I was only telling the truth.

"Our wages are as good as most," he replied sharply. "You should understand this."

"I've only just started here, sir."

"You should have been told."

I nodded, afraid to say any more in case I said the wrong thing. He went on about the fact that if a girl earned less than twelve shillings a week, it was her own fault for not working the full hours, and for taking time off for trivial reasons or because of natural laziness.

Then he said, "Did this journalist mention Annie Besant ... or maybe a man named Stead?"

"No, sir."

"What about Hunt or Sidney Webb?"

I shook my head. It sounded too risky to agree to Annie Besant though the journalist had mentioned her. It sounded like a trick question.

He sighed heavily. "Someone is spreading malicious rumours that we fine the girls for the slightest misdemeanour. Have you ever been fined?"

"No sir, but I know a girl who–"

"There you are, you see? Nothing more than rumours. Mr Bryant and Mr May are excellent owners and have the welfare of the workforce at heart." He consulted his notes. "And as to the requests for a separate room for you to eat in – have you ever requested such a thing?"

I looked at him blankly. A room to eat our food in? No one had said anything to me about it. We ate in the yard or at our benches if it rained.

"I can see by your expression, Miss Finch, that you know nothing about such a request." He wrote on the paper again and glanced at the clock.

Had we finished the conversation, I wondered and crossed my fingers hopefully.

"You'd better get back to your work, Miss Finch. I shall overlook your behaviour this time because you are new here, but please understand that I shall not be so lenient in the future if I hear further news that you have been indiscreet and allowed your tongue to run away with you. Don't be led astray by pie and mash, Miss Finch – with or without gravy!" He peered over the top of his spectacles at me and I think he almost smiled. "You are on the Bryant & May payroll and, in this somewhat deprived area, I would expect you to be grateful for regular work. That will be all."

I fled down the stairs with my heart still racing. Even now, writing about it in this diary, my hand is shaking.

Wednesday, 13th June

Off work today. Ma had a sick headache so Annie and I looked after Dora and made matchboxes all day until we ran out of paste and didn't have enough money to buy more, so I sent Annie to Kitty's to borrow some. She was a long time coming back because she saw an organ grinder playing music and he had a monkey who held out his paw for pennies. Annie stopped to dance (as well as she can) with the other girls until she tripped and cut her hand on a piece of broken bottle and came home in tears.

"Serves you right," I told her. "You were wasting time and time's money."

She sulked all evening until Ma got up and gave her a clip round the ear for moping about.

Thursday, 14th June

This morning we started work ten minutes late because we all had to listen to a boring lady doctor telling us about phossy jaw and how we wouldn't get it if we went regularly to the dentist's room for treatment. I was in the second row from the front and every now and then she seemed to speak directly to me.

"If you get decay in your tooth, it can be stopped with a filling so it won't get any worse and you won't have to have the tooth out," she told us. "We have the best up-to-date equipment – a drill worked by clockwork – that speeds up the treatment. It's when you have a decayed tooth taken out that the trouble starts. Phosphorous gets into the raw hole and ends up in the bone and when that happens the entire jawbone becomes infected and that is very serious indeed." She drew a long breath. "There is no cure for the disease known as phossy jaw."

She paused to let that sink in and the audience was very still. Most of us knew someone who had died from the disease but the last thing we wanted to do was think about it. I was trying my hardest not to think about it and was looking at the doctor instead. She was small and thin and had a white coat on over her clothes, and her hair was hidden under a white cap. She wasn't very pretty but she wore shiny brown leather shoes with a buttoned strap that would have cost a week of my wages. If ever I'm rich, I'll buy some just like hers.

She went on earnestly. "The jawbone disintegrates, affecting your speech and the way you eat and there's no stopping it... A filling in the early stages..."

Yes, I thought, but the few girls who go to the dentist for a filling say it hurts so much, it makes your eyes water with the pain of it. And it's quicker to have it out. No wonder nobody chooses a filling. That's why my sister Ellie had her tooth out and got the white phosphorous in her jaw. At first we didn't notice anything but then her gum was sore and her jaw started to ache and her teeth got a bit loose. When it got really bad her jawbone went all crumbly and out of shape and made her look ugly. She couldn't speak properly – she just mumbled – and she couldn't chew her food. Poor Ellie. She was a good sister to me. I miss her.

Patty yawned very loudly to let the doctor know we'd heard it all before and this talk was costing us money in lost wages. The doctor asked if we had any questions and someone shouted, "Yes. When can we get back to making matches?" and we all laughed and she went a bit red. Nobody wanted to waste time asking her anything so she said we could get back to our benches. We all muttered and grumbled as we left the room to let her know we weren't very pleased.

I haven't told Ma about being sent for by the manager 'cos I'm sure she'd say it was all my fault. She thinks we're being feather-bedded compared with her days as a costermonger. She and her pa worked all the hours it was light, come rain or shine, summer or winter, trudging the filthy streets, dodging between the horse traffic and fending off the lads who would snatch the apples and scarper, thinking it a big joke. She thinks factory work with a roof over our heads is a snip and that we girls are ungrateful and don't know when we're well off.

I wonder if I'll see that young man again. I can sometimes taste that pie and mash and wouldn't say no to another plateful.

A bit of good news. Patty is walking out with Mr Stringer, the nice foreman who isn't married. If they get married, she might ask me to the wedding – but goodness only knows what I could wear.

Friday, 15th June

Bit of a do today at the factory when a bell started to ring. Deafening it was and we all looked at each other until Patty said it must be the fire alarm and could any of us remember the drill about how to get out of the building. We all started to panic but then Mr Sugden started shouting that it wasn't a real fire but a drill. We all had to line up at the window because our room is on the first floor and we had to pretend the stairs were on fire. The bell went on ringing and it was really getting on my nerves, and some of the girls were upset, even though it was only a practice. It took ages to get everyone lined up at the window and Sugden was rushing around like a headless chicken. Then I found myself in the line at the window. There was a long ladder going down to the yard and we had to climb out over the window sill in our long skirts and go down. It was quite exciting.

But it wasn't as exciting as it was for the girls on the second floor. They didn't have a long enough ladder so had to climb out and slide down a long white thing like a strong narrow sheet. I think it was called a chute.

I would have been all right on the ladder, except that Patty was coming down above me a bit too fast and stepped on my head so I had to let go of the ladder to push her foot away and fell off. Luckily I was only about eight rungs up and so I didn't kill myself but it shook me up and I grazed my hands and hurt my knees, and Patty got a ticking-off from the man in charge of the ladder, which served her right.

The whole thing wasted a lot of time and one of the girls asked Sugden if we would lose money because of the drill.

"'Ow the 'ell do I know?" he snapped. "Just do what you're told and keep your mouth shut!"

He really is a surly devil. I like to think that if I met him by the river one dark night when he was drunk, I'd push the wretch into the water and watch him drown. I'm sure nobody would miss him.

Saturday, 16th June

I went out early today to fetch some potatoes and carrots from the market, pushing my way through the usual crowd, half-deafened by the shouts of people hawking their wares, and trying to ignore the beggars who lined the pavements. A man playing a fiddle wore a cardboard notice round his neck with the word BLIND scrawled on it in charcoal. There was a small girl with bare feet and dirty blond curls, holding out a chipped mug. Beyond her a woman with one leg sat on an upturned fish basket holding out both calloused hands while tears trickled down her cheeks. A young boy sold Lucifer matches.

Those people always depress me so I hurried past to do my shopping. On the way back I stopped on the corner of Fairfield Road, where there was a bit of a crowd and a lady and a man were standing on boxes and talking about the workers being treated like slaves. I thought they meant us girls but then realized they were talking about the miners, dockers, seamen and engineers. She said they were being paid a pittance, whatever that is.

A costermonger was standing next to me with a barrow full of walnuts. "They're right," he said. "We'll be having a revolution soon. You mark my words. People won't put up with it." He was short and chunky with a skimpy beard, and made me think of a gnome.

"A revolution?" I asked. "Are you sure?"

"Sure as eggs is eggs! Oh yes! And I for one will be glad of it." He thrust out a grimy hand and I shook it obligingly. "Fred Duffy at your service."

"Oh. Yes. I'm Florence Finch."

"You want to know about revolution, Fred Duffy's your man! Chuck out the government, I say. Get rid of the stinking rich and give all their money to the poor! Chop off a few heads while we're at it!" He grinned horribly. "The French had the right idea!" He drew the side of his hand across his throat. "We could do with a guillotine in this country!"

I have to admit he made me nervous. "What about the queen?" I asked. I can't imagine the world without our noble queen in it. We don't see her very often, in fact I've never met Queen Victoria, but I know she's there, being victorious, ruling over us and being glorious and everything.

"Her too!" cried Mr Duffy. "What does she care for the likes of us, eh? Not a blooming sausage. Not one jot or tittle!" Reluctantly he prepared to move on, pushing his small barrow and shouting, "Walnuts, finest walnuts! Sixteen a penny!"

A woman next to me shook her head. "Dunno what the world's coming to! All these strikes and what 'ave you. 'Ow we s'posed to eat with the menfolk on strike? Where's it all going to end?" She moved her basket to the other arm and I saw that it held a couple of muddy potatoes and three small herrings. "I've got an 'usband and five kids to feed. My Albert goes on strike over my dead body!"

A man next to her nodded. "I blame the government, I

36

do. If I was the queen, I'd sack the lot of them. Sitting in their big houses and lording it over the likes of us 'ard-working folks! Talk about sweated labour! It's a disgrace, that's what it is!"

I thought it best not to mention the revolution and people having their heads chopped off.

The woman jerked a thumb in the direction of the speakers. "These two are stirring it up good and proper. Troublemakers, that's what they are. 'E's Sidney Webb..." She jerked her thumb in his direction. "And she's Annie Besant."

Annie Besant! There it was again – the woman the manager had asked me about ... and the one the young journalist had mentioned. It made me feel guilty somehow so I hurried away.

Imagine how I felt when I found that same journalist waiting at home for me! The cheek of it! He was sitting in Pa's chair and Ma was treating him like bloomin' royalty. Annie was still pasting on labels but Ma had stopped to entertain the visitor. I glanced round the room, which as usual smelled of matchbox paste, and the breakfast cups and plates were still in the sink. I don't know what he thought.

Ma was looking flustered. "For goodness sake, Flo, poor Mr Lytton has been waiting ages," she said. "He wants to speak to you. He says he wants to show you something."

Annie was also gawping at him as though he'd just come down off the nearest cloud. Baby Dora was bawling but nobody took any notice of her. We usually give her a spoonful of Godfrey's Cordial to quieten her, even though Emma says it's got opium in it (which is a drug) and you shouldn't give it to babies. Emma says that they give their babies "penny sticks" to suck on. But how do they know what's in a penny stick? Their first baby died for no good reason so they don't know everything.

Mr Lytton stood up, handed back his cup, then pulled a newspaper from his pocket and unfolded it... "This is what I wrote about you," he said proudly and began to read aloud.

'A young lady, who shall be nameless, spoke to me about her working life as a match girl in the Fairfield Road factory at Bow–'

"Oh no!" I cried. "You never put my name in the paper? Oh, tell me you didn't!"

Ma was as white as a sheet and my heart was thumping.

"I didn't," he insisted. It says 'A young lady who shall be nameless... No name! See?'

"No name?" said Ma. "Well, thank the Lord for that! You have got some sense! " and let out a long breath.

I sat down on the wonky chair and stared at Mr Lytton. Annie's mouth was open and she was blinking the way she does when she's scared. Ma gave her a nudge and said, "Get on with them boxes!"

Mr Lytton went on reading aloud, struggling a bit against the noise the baby was making.

'It seems she works as a packer for around twelve shillings a week but this is reduced if she takes time off for whatever reason. She enjoys the company of the other young women who work alongside her at their workbench but feels that some of the foremen are rather hard on them…'

I protested that I didn't say that exactly but he said it wouldn't matter because he didn't use my name to save me any embarrassment.

Suddenly the light dawned. "You didn't know my name!" I said. "How could you use it?"

Without thinking, Ma leaned forward and slapped my arm. "Mind your manners, Flossie!"

It didn't hurt but it made me feel stupid in front of Mr Lytton. By this time it was beginning to dawn on him that me being in the paper wasn't making me happy so he rolled up the newspaper and stuffed it back in his pocket. He said he was sorry if he'd upset me. He had just wanted to thank me for helping him with the article and would I like to meet him later and we'd go the pie shop again. Before I could say no Ma piped up.

"Course she'd like to," and gave me one of her looks, so I said yes and we agreed on seven o'clock.

After he'd gone Ma went on about what a suitable young man he was, attractive, nicely spoken – and was he married? I said I didn't know. "He was careful not to mention your name," she reminded me, "and he's very generous. He's taken a shine to you, and no mistake!"

Annie asked, "Don't you want to go the pie shop again?"

I wavered then.

"He'd be a real catch," Ma said. "Your pa would approve."

Just then Annie reminded me that Alfred was coming at half past seven to take me for a walk in the park, if it didn't turn foggy. (London fogs are full of soot and mess your clothes up something terrible. They're so thick, we call them "pea-soupers") Ma thought fast and said I couldn't turn Mr Lytton down because he was such a gentleman.

"I don't want to lie to Alfred," I said uncertainly.

"Well, I'll lie for you!" she insisted.

She would tell Alfred I was in bed with a bellyache and couldn't go with him. By that time I was persuaded and so busy wondering if I could find a new ribbon for my hat that I didn't give poor Alfred another thought.

Course it was just my luck later on that as we came out of the pie shop we bumped into Alfred – and he was with a girl with ginger hair! I don't know who got the worst shock – him or me. They were arm in arm and laughing but when he saw me it wiped the smile off his face. He said he thought I was ill in bed with a pain and I told him I was but it went away very suddenly.

"And who's this, then?" he demanded, surly like, glaring at Mr Lytton.

I said grandly, "Mr Lytton is a journalist writing about factories for a magazine." That certainly made them stare. "And who's this carrot top?" I asked, glaring at the girl. She was quite pretty, with a turned-up nose and freckles. I didn't recognise her from the factory so maybe she isn't a match girl.

"Who're you calling names?" she said and stepped forward with her fists up. I thought she was going to hit me so I put mine up but Mr Lytton grabbed her arm and then Alfred grabbed his arm and before I knew it the two men were scrapping and landing punches. Alfred fell over and as he went down he bumped into a woman who was passing and she started yelling at him and calling us hooligans and when Alfred got up her husband knocked him down again and a bit of a crowd formed and started egging them on. Cheering and suchlike. I was yelling at them to stop but Carrot Top was urging Alfred to "Give 'im one!" – meaning Mr Lytton.

Someone blew a whistle and, before you could say "knife", a policeman appeared at the end of the road so we all took off, me and Mr Lytton in one direction and Alfred and Carrot Top in the other.

We had a good laugh about it and Mr Lytton asked me to call him Jake, because his name's Jacob, so I said he could call me Florence instead of Miss Finch. Bit of a turn up for the books, really, I thought.

When I got home Kitty was there with a bag of peppermints and news that the factory was taking on more girls, but then somehow we all got to talking about Grandpa, and Ma said that he used to write in a diary every day but when they cleared out his room, it was nowhere to be found. I said nothing because I didn't want them to know I had it. They might be wanting to read what Grandpa had written and then they might read my pages as well. I mean, a diary has to be private, doesn't it?

Monday, 18th June

There's a rumour going round the factory that some new workers, who mostly seem to be Scottish, have been brought in specially and are being paid lower wages than us. Patty thinks that at some time they'll expect all of us to take less money and if we refuse, they'll give us the sack and bring in more girls from Scotland.

Is it true? I don't understand it. Jake says it's the bosses trying to grind the faces of the poor, but I thought Bryant & May was a good firm to work for so I wonder if he's got it wrong. Either that or it's not such a good firm.

I know we get less work anyway in the summer but Patty says that's because people use less matches when it's warm weather so Bryant & May sell less. Lots of the girls go off hop-picking in Kent and Emma's going to work in a factory that makes jam, but I'll stay on at Bryant & May's. If they cut back on our hours, I'll help Ma with making the matchboxes at home.

Jake says there's going to be problems this summer because it's been a bad year for fruit, which means the jam factories might not need so many extra workers. He says there's going to be too little work and people will go hungry. And get angry. Civil unrest. That's what he calls it.

He took me to a meeting in Hyde Park, where there was a demonstration against Bryant & May and all the other factories that make matches, and there was a giant matchbox being carried around and on it there was a picture of a clergyman saying his prayers. I had to laugh but Jake said it was serious. The clergyman was thanking God for the high dividends he was getting on his Bryant & May shares. I couldn't understand the argument and told him I didn't really care but Jake said I should make more of an effort. I was very offended and stalked off in a sulk, but he came chasing after me and bought me a toffee apple to say he was sorry.

But then he complained that I didn't understand things about social justice and should show more interest. I felt quite cross about that. To my mind, he doesn't understand much about the match industry. "You don't care about our side of it," I told him, "and you don't ask. You should make more of an effort! It's very interesting, the match industry."

"Interesting? How exactly?" he asked.

He can be very annoying. I searched my mind for something to tell him. "There's all sorts of matches," I began. "Some special matches for when it's windy – they're called wind matches because they don't blow out so easily. And there's fusees, which are for lighting cigars because they don't have a flame but a slow burn…"

To be fair, he was beginning to look interested.

I went on, determined to prove my point. "There's some boxes we produce with "Defence not Defiance" written on them with a picture of three soldiers but I'm not sure what that's about. Then there's paraffin matches – they're damp-proof, see. Then there are wax vestas and six-inch spills…"

He asked if there were any matches made for when you don't actually want to light anything, and for a few seconds I thought about it quite seriously until I realized he was making fun of me. I gave him a push and then he pulled my hair and I pinched his arm, and then he kissed me. Not quite a romantic kiss but it was definitely a kiss and not a peck on the cheek.

I stared at him. "You can't do that! We're not walking out together."

"I know but ... we could, couldn't we?"

I thought he was pulling my leg. "My ma would go mad!" I told him. I meant mad with excitement.

"So would mine!" He didn't mean that. He meant his mother wouldn't think me suitable.

I shrugged.

"Best not, then," he said.

I had a vision of his mother, all prim and elegant with a rolled-up parasol, learning that her son was walking out with a factory girl from Bryant & Mays. He was looking rather worried and I knew he'd made a mistake. Silly fool had kissed me on the spur of the moment. He's nearly twenty but still larking about and not at all grown up. I felt rather sorry for him.

I bit back my hurt and smiled instead. "They send our matches to places like India and China," I said doggedly. "The Indian ones have a picture of an elephant on the box... And there are perfumed matches and suchlike." My face was stiff with smiling. "You should write about all that in your article, Jake Lytton, instead of going on about strikes all the time."

"So you girls wouldn't come out on strike?" he asked.

"Did I say that?" I tossed my head. "We might." We had thought about it. Of course we had. We had complaints and we wouldn't say no to better wages. Yes, I thought. One day we might well do more than think!

Wednesday, 20th June

I thought that Jake probably lived in a house and I didn't like to ask but he told me this morning that he lives in rented rooms with his widowed mother. He says they used to be worth a few bob because his pa was a train driver and his ma teaches the piano, but his pa died of a seizure two years ago. Jake and his ma still live in the same rooms but now they have a lodger to help pay the rent. Their spare room is let to an elderly spinster who takes in ironing to make a living. Jake says the smell of the ironing is awful but I told him, "We've got the smell of matchbox paste and that's awful too."

The world is full of foul smells! Or is it just London? Or all towns? The countryside might be better but I've never been there so I don't know. But they've got cows and horses and sheep and pigs, and they must smell a bit. Probably a lot! But the girls at the factory who go hop-picking say the hops smell nice and there are lots of fruit trees and fresh air, and they don't have horrible yellow fogs so it can't be too bad.

Jake wants to write a long article about what it's like to be a match girl working in a factory. He wants to ask me questions about it and especially about the phossy jaw, but I don't want him to get me in any more trouble. Being sent for by the manager once was bad enough. I don't want it to happen again. I'd get a bad reputation. Jake says he won't use my name in the article and if I say yes he'll ask his ma if I can go to their rooms and have tea and a slice of cake. Ma carries on about "my big chance" and if I don't go she says she'll never speak to me again. So I suppose I will!

Thursday, 21st June

Jake's ma is really nice, even though she is a bit prissy. She can't help that and I don't blame her. She was wearing a blue skirt with a white blouse and pretty lace collar and she had a very clean gingham apron over her skirt and tied at the back. I was glad she's never seen me at my workbench at the factory!

I can see the likeness between them. Mrs Lytton and Jake, I mean. Same nice eyes and broad forehead and warm smile. I wondered why she only had one child (Jake) but thought it might sound rather rude so I didn't ask. The rooms are in a pleasant street. The hall floor has white and black tiles but the smell from the lodger's room was hot and steamy from the ironing, and Jake hustled me into the front room and shut the door.

They have a piano! They have to so that Mrs Lytton can give her lessons. I've never actually seen a piano before – just the organs the organ-grinders use – and it was beautiful. The keys are creamy white and there are some black keys, and the rest is very shiny wood, very polished. When I admired it Mrs Lytton played me a little tune called "Frère Jacques", which is French for Brother Jack, so now I can speak a bit of French, which might come in useful one day if I meet a French man called Jack. You never know.

We had a cup of tea in beautiful cups with roses on them and there was a teapot that matched and a bowl for the sugar and a little jug for the milk – all with roses – and we had tiny sandwiches with potted meat in them. There was a homemade cake with caraway seeds and I had two slices. It was quite wonderful.

Then Mrs Lytton said she had a girl coming for a piano lesson so Jake and I had to move into the kitchen, where the smell of the lodger's ironing was worse.

Jake told me that there was talk of the Salvation Army building a new match factory and that they would be using only red phosphorous in their matches. He said that red phosphorous wasn't dangerous like the white kind and added, "So maybe, you could go and work there instead."

To my surprise I felt a rush of loyalty towards Bryant & May. "I expect we'll start using the red sort as well," I said. "I wouldn't leave all my friends. Anyway, I like it there."

"As long as you girls are safe." He smiled as he sharpened his pencil and then got down to work. "Question number one, Floss –"

"If you don't call me Florence, I won't answer," I told him.

"Sorry – Florence." He grinned. "I saw a girl in the street yesterday whose jaw was a funny shape and very swollen. I asked her about it and she tried to speak but could only mumble. Was that phossy jaw?"

I nodded. Memories of Ellie rushed into my head. Ellie, fit and well, taking me to school for my first day. Ellie bringing me a stray kitten to care for (even though it disappeared again after a week) ... and then Ellie with her face all swollen, crying the night before she died.

Jake asked, "Do you know how it's caused?"

I nodded but said nothing because it seemed like bad luck to keep talking about it.

"Phosphorous vapour gets into the gums," he said, "and

then the jaw starts to crumble because the bone breaks up."

I nodded again but I hated the questions. If he already knew all this, why ask me, I thought.

He said, "It can damage your brain. Did you know that?"

I shook my head. I didn't want to know any more about it. I had lived my whole life with the shadow of it hanging over me. Had Ellie's brain been damaged? How would we have known if it was, I wondered. Should I tell Ma?

Jake seemed to be fascinated by the whole thing. He said that after a certain time there would be so much phosphorous in a jaw that the bones would glow in the dark!

It sounded frightful. Like a ghost or something. "Ellie's didn't." I told him.

He asked me what she actually died of and I said blood poisoning because that's what the doctor told Ma only he also used a long word which I can't remember but it started with "s"

"Septicaemia?" he asked.

"I suppose so." My voice was shaking by this time and I thought I might break down and cry so he said he'd finished with the questions and thanked me for my help.

When I went home I told Ma all about the visit but left out the bit about the phossy jaw. I didn't want two of us crying ourselves to sleep that night.

Friday, 22nd June

The postman brought me a letter from Alfred but for a few minutes I was afraid to open it. Inside there was a piece of paper torn from a notebook. It said "Dear Miss Finch, You told me a lie and who was that man? Dont bother to tell me. I wont care if I never see you again. Your obedient servant, Alfred."

I wished then that it hadn't happened the way it did. I wished it had been a love letter. I've never had one and it would have been exciting, even if it was only Alfred. But it wasn't a love letter and I felt wretched because I had told him a lie, which wasn't very nice of me. I was sort of disappointed in myself and I tried to blame Jake for asking me to go and have tea with his mother, but it wasn't really his fault. It was mine. And Ma's. I read the letter again and took some comfort from the fact that Alfred didn't say Carrot Top was prettier than me – even though she is.

I wondered whether to tell Ma about the letter but decided to think it over first. Maybe I should answer it and say I was sorry, but if I did he might show the letter to Carrot Top and I'd hate that because they'd laugh about me together.

I wondered what Mrs Lytton thought when she saw the bruise on Jake's face, which he got in the scrap. I hope he didn't tell the truth because then she'd think me a bad influence and I might not get invited to tea again. I had a scratch down my face but I told Ma it was from a stray cat I picked up.

Ma's in a funny mood today because Pa's ship has docked – three days ago – and she's only just heard about it and wants to know where he is and if he's spending all his wages in the beer rooms, gambling it away on the card games he loves. I said we should go and look for him but Ma's too stubborn. I might go and look for him tomorrow without telling her. If he's drunk, the news about Grandpa dying will soon sober him up.

Kitty came round and upset me by saying that *The Link* magazine is produced by something called the Fabian Society and they are fighting for social change, which means looking out for people like me who get exploited by the owners of the factories.

"There's trouble brewing, Flo," she said, "and they stir it up and make things worse. So you want to be careful about young Jake. He could get you into trouble, writing stuff like he does. You could get the sack, being seen with him."

My heart sank. Ma must have told her about me being sent to the manager.

Kitty insisted that people who read those sort of articles

get all steamed up and that's how strikes start and then everyone has no work, which means no money and terrible hardship.

Ma was listening unhappily. "So what happens if the factory is closed down by a strike? Do they all starve?"

Kitty shrugged. "Maybe. Or they have to find other work or go begging."

Ma's eyes widened. "Begging? No girl of mine's going to go begging!" So now she's telling me to stay away from Jake, in case he gets me into trouble. "You get back together with Alfred," she advised. "He may not be God's gift to women and he can be a miserable whotsit but he's a decent enough lad."

What could I say? I couldn't tell her about the fight and the letter from Alfred. She had enough worries wondering about Pa. Why is life so difficult?

Saturday, 23rd June

Thank the Lord! Ma's happy again. Pa turned up yesterday evening (with his usual beard. That will soon come off in the halfpenny barbers!) with his wages and presents for all of us. It seemed that he was ill with a fever on the return journey and still very weak when they docked and two other men were also ill so they all stayed on board the *Tally Rose* while she was being unloaded.

Pa looks very thin and pale (and, to my eyes, much older). To see him now you would never think that, in his younger days, he used to box with his bare fists and men used to wager money on him winning which he often did and came away with the prize money!

Ma clung to him speechlessly the moment he walked through the door but not for long because she hates to show her feelings. Then she patted his arm, saying she will fatten him up again before he goes back to sea.

Pa gave Ma a bit of lace, enough for a narrow collar, and she can't stop admiring it. Baby Dora's got a rattle, Annie's got a little wooden doll and I have a bright cotton kerchief to tie back my hair or tie it round my neck. It's all flowery and too good for every day so I shall keep it for high days and holidays.

Then, of course, we had to tell Pa the sad news about Grandpa, and his face fell. He covered his eyes with his hands and none of us knew what to say to comfort him.

"I never got to say goodbye!" he said, over and over. "I should have been here!"

Then he asked about paying for the funeral and did we owe any money? Ma told him about the money she got from selling Grandpa's furniture and he was pleased that was settled and told Ma she'd "done well".

Then he talked a bit about Grandpa when he was younger, when Grandma was still alive. And we remembered absent friends and loved ones, which included our dear Ellie! Now and then Pa seemed overcome and wiped away a tear, but at last he cheered up and sent me and Annie out with a pocketful of change to buy us something to eat "to remember the dear departed".

"And send 'Coalie' round, Flo, with a hod full of coals for the hot water!" he added.

Pa always looks forward to a decent bath when he comes home.

Having found the hod carrier and given him the message and our address, Annie and I elbowed our way through the crowds in the market, enjoying the hustle and bustle and the shouts of the street-sellers. We listened to a man singing 'Duck-legged Dick Had a Donkey' which is Annie's favourite ballad, and gave a ha'penny to the organ grinder further along because I couldn't resist the monkey's tiny outstretched paw. There was a juggler and an acrobat and even a dancing dog with a bright yellow collar ... and then I caught sight of a child of about four, holding out a mug. I recognized her from a previous trip to the market. She was very dirty and her feet were still bare and I decided to give her a ha'penny, but just then the church clock struck eight and we realized how much time we had wasted. Annie dragged me off in the opposite direction and we hastily set about buying our dinner before the best bargains had gone.

It's never easy, choosing from so much.

"Three Yarmouth bloaters for a penny!"

"Pickled whelks, fresh today!"

"Hot sheep's trotters, penny a pair!"

Everyone yelling, dogs barking, live chickens squawking – and a policeman keeping a watchful eye out for thieves and pickpockets.

Annie begged to be allowed to visit the penny concert so after a short argument I gave in, on the understanding that she didn't tell. Ma says the penny concerts are a scam and not worth the money. Annie, delighted, disappeared through a shabby doorway with her penny and came out a few moments later. "It was a man singing," she told me, trying to hide her disappointment. "He had a top hat and a fancy waistcoat, and he stood on a crate and sang a song about a runaway pig!"

"How many people were in the audience?"

"Only me."

I rolled my eyes. "And how many verses did he sing?"

"Only one."

"Told you so!" I grinned.

We ended up with meat puddings, hot green peas and baked potatoes, which we wrapped in a cloth and carried home before they could get cold.

We had a great supper, happy and cheerful, and I managed to forget my troubles for the rest of the evening. I lay in bed smiling up into the darkness. I always feel safer when Pa's home. I don't know why, but I do.

Sunday, 24th June

Grandpa used to say that "Bad news travels fast!" and it certainly seems that way. Kitty rushed round this morning with a magazine .

"A ha'penny well spent!" she cried.

Ma had her head under the sink, looking to see if we'd had any luck with the mousetrap overnight, and Annie was buttering bread for our breakfast. I was feeding baby Dora with warm bread and water. Pa was still in bed and I guessed Ma was hoping he would stay there because he disapproves of Kitty and finds her presence irritating.

Ma told Kitty about him having had the fever on the journey home and still recovering but Kitty wasn't even interested. They just don't like each other. Without bothering to sit down, Kitty struck a dramatic pose and began.

"Listen to this article, you lot!" She waved the magazine. "Everyone's saying it's explosive!"

"What?" cried Annie, turning from the bread and butter to gaze in horror at Kitty. "Explosives?"

"I don't mean explosives," Kitty said, annoyed by the interruption. "I mean explosive ideas – in the article." She rolled her eyes and sighed.

I said, "Go on, Kitty."

The article, apparently, was entitled 'White Slavery' in London and was all about us. Someone called Clementina Black had been writing against the government for letting people exploit the poor. She declared that some of the match girls at our factory were only being paid four shillings a week, while the shareholders, who had bought shares in the company for £5 each, could now cash them in for more than £18 each.

Trying to sound bright, I asked, "Is that too much, then?"

Kitty snorted. "It's a bloomin' lot, if you ask me! Too bloomin' much! That's what they call grinding the faces of the poor, Flo! People like us, the workers, get a pittance for our labours and the rich investors do nothing but put a bit of money in and get a big percentage on their investments. That means a big handout! Lots of profit. Tons of cash. We're working our fingers to the bone and making them rich!"

Her voice shrill and her eyes blazing, Kitty told us in no uncertain terms that it was a scandal and a disgrace and the Fabian Society, (who speak up for the downtrodden like us) were up in arms.

"All the newspapers are full of it," she said, her face flushed with excitement. "There's going to be a campaign and demonstrations in Hyde Park so everyone can go and listen. Banners and speakers – the lot! I expect it'll be Annie Besant and Sidney Webb. If the worst happens there might be a riot, with police on horseback."

Kitty ran out of breath, took another and went on. "And clashes! There'll be clashes that's what people are saying. A breakdown of law and order. It might even lead to another strike."

Before we could ask any questions, she rushed away to pass on the news to other friends and we were left looking at each other doubtfully. I said that if we went on strike we'd get no wages. Pa came in then, still in his nightshirt, and asked if Kitty had gone.

We told him the news and he looked worried. Ma said that she didn't want me to go on strike but Pa pointed out that a strike meant "one out, all out!" and if the workers withdrew their labour, the factory would be closed down and the gates locked. So I'd have to join the strike, whether I wanted to or not.

It sounded very serious and my heart seemed to beat a

little faster. Suddenly I imagined myself begging barefoot on the street, with my hair all tousled, looking sad and pitiful with tears in the brown eyes Alfred sets so much store by, (or used to). I thought I would make a wonderfully tragic figure – a beautiful, heart-rending creature begging for pennies. I wondered how generous passers-by would be. I thought I might do quite well...

Then, quite suddenly, I was hating myself for not helping the little barefoot girl I had seen again at the market the evening before. How terrible it must be, I thought guiltily, to depend on the kindness of strangers, especially when they can't even be bothered to give you a ha'penny but go wandering off in search of a nice dinner instead.

"I'm so sorry!" I whispered.

But then, remembering my own possible predicament, I realized that if all the match girls from Bryant & May were begging on the street at the same time, there would be hundreds of us all looking tragic and heartrending. Maybe I wouldn't do so well. None of us would.

"Do you go on strike on your ship, Pa?" asked Annie.

That made him laugh. I always loved to see him happy so I smiled as well and Ma said, "Don't give him any ideas, Annie!"

Pa pulled Annie on to his lap and hugged her. He said, "If we went on strike at sea, it would be called a mutiny and we'd get into very serious trouble."

That worried me. "Will we get into serious trouble, if we go on strike?" I asked.

We had all been talking about going on strike and some of the girls were mad for the idea and thought it would be a good lark, but I worried about it. One of the older women, called Aggie said, she thought Bryant & May were asking for trouble and why did we have to wait? We should just go ahead and do it! And Marge, who works opposite me, said we should go to the managers and make demands and if they won't agree then we should all walk out. But I dared not let on to Ma and Pa. Ma would have a fit, even if Pa understood.

"I don't know," he said in answer to my question." "You couldn't all be sacked or there'd be no more matches produced and no more money for the shareholders." He scratched his head. "Sometimes they get up a strike fund and wealthy people with kind hearts give money, and then it's shared out among the strikers so they can pay their rent and not starve. But not always." He rubbed his eyes and sank on to his chair. "Pour us a cup of tea, Ma, for pity's sake." he said. "A nice homecoming this has turned out to be. My own daughter might be going on strike! This is a rum go and no mistake!"

Monday, 25th June

There's a rumour going round that the management are trying to persuade some of the girls to sign papers saying that they like working for Bryant & May and the foremen are kind to them, and that they all earn good money. But as far as I can find out, no one has agreed to sign and the managers are not at all pleased.

Mr Sugden is trying his best to find out what's going on and getting very bad tempered. He fined one of the girls for swearing. She says he's lying but she still had to pay twopence and all the girls are giving him the "cold shoulder".

Another girl – a woman called Ella Copsley who works upstairs from us, dropped an armful of matchboxes and accused the foreman of deliberately tripping her with his foot, which he denies. He has sent her home so she will lose an afternoon's pay.

We're all up in arms about the slightest things and it feels as though war has been declared between "them and us". Patty says it's because the newspapers are taking sides – some are for us and some are for the management. Jake says it's going to end in a strike and he can't wait for it to happen! Trust him.

Emma wasn't at work so I went round afterwards to see if she was all right and if she had signed anything. No one has asked me to sign anything but that may be because I haven't been here long so have very little experience and my opinion doesn't count for anything.

Emma was looking very dejected, with a swollen face and raging toothache, which made me feel very nervous as memories of my sister Ellie rushed into my mind. Her mother said that if she doesn't want to go to the dentist at the factory she might have to go to the one in the High Street to have the tooth out. To have it out! That terrified me and I desperately tried to make her change her mind and go to the factory dentist for a filling.

"I can't face it," Emma told me. "The moment I set foot in the room, I want to run away."

"But you've never had a tooth stopped," I argued. "They just fill up the hole."

Emma shook her head. "I went in with Clara when she had hers done because she was scared to go in on her own. They use a clockwork drill to get rid of the decay and it's horrible. By the time she came out, she was close to fainting. All upset and wobbly at the knees." She shuddered at the memory. "And all that poking and prodding. Having it out will be quicker and then it's all over with. It's at the back of my mouth so the gap won't show."

I almost reminded her about what happened to

my sister but somehow it didn't seem right. A bit like preaching. So instead I told her what was happening at work and she replied, "Then I'm well out of it!"

Then she said she'd seen Carrot Top walking out hand-in-hand with someone who was not Alfred. I was secretly pleased to hear it but pretended I was not interested. I shrugged and said, "Good luck to the pair of them!" But then I had an awful thought, that maybe Alfred and Emma would get together. I didn't want to ask outright and wondered if Emma would tell me if they were ever walking out, but she said nothing more. I remembered her dropping the violets into Grandpa's grave. Can I trust her, I wonder?

Her mother came in to tell us that some shareholders, who thought we girls were being ill-treated by the management, had sold their shares as a protest and that was a bad sign for Bryant & May. She said, "Lord help the boxmakers who do the 'home' work, if it comes to a strike. They hardly earn enough to live on as it is, poor souls. Less than threepence for a gross of boxes and they have to pay for the string and paste out of that!"

Emma and I looked at each other.

Her mother went on. "They'll be starving before the week's out – or knocking on the door of the "house".

By "house" she meant the workhouse and I began to feel a bit panicky as I thought about it. Truth to tell, I felt a cold shiver run up my spine. Life was hard enough without a strike making things worse for everyone. The workhouse is a very strict place and the master doesn't like giving people money to help them through short periods of distress. He likes to say "take the house" which means that if you go in, you have to stay in. Then you are made to do hard unpleasant work, such as picking oakum (which means untangling tarry rope) or, if you are a man you have to break up stones for use on the roads. They are given poor meals and a bed in return. People say it's worse than prison. That's why everyone dreads it so.

Tuesday, 26th June

Pa looks much better now that he's had his beard shaved off and he's had some good food to build him up. But he's worrying about the possible strike at the factory and the lack of money when – if – it happens. We won't be unable to make up the money with "home" work because there won't be a need for the boxes if the factory has stopped making the matches. Pa says he will try and get a job at the docks but we all know it's not very likely because there are hundreds of men wanting such jobs and not nearly enough work for all of them. Truth to tell, I'm getting heartily weary of the word "strike"!

Wednesday, 27th June

Nothing's changed at work except that Patty says someone's tried to count the girls who came down from Scotland to work here and it might be more than fifty or even a hundred – more than we thought. And they are getting paid less than us. What does it mean? I'm beginning to suspect that if we go on strike, the Scottish girls will carry on doing our jobs but working longer hours and getting paid overtime or something. Then the strike would not be so effective. Who can you trust? I'm keeping the idea to myself. No point in making matters worse.

Friday, 29th June

Stayed home yesterday and today to look after Ma and baby Dora because Ma is in bed with a sick headache and

Pa is out looking for work. He didn't bring home as much money as usual because he was laid up ill on the ship so wasn't paid any money for those days.

Someone posted a card through the letter box and I think it might have been Jake because I haven't seen or heard from him lately. It was a picture of a rose but there was no message. Or it might be from Alfred. Anyway it's nice and romantic.

Ma said jokingly, "How d'you know it's for you, Flo? Maybe I have a secret admirer!" and Pa said, "If you have, I'll black his eye for him!" He's not usually a violent man but he might do it. He doesn't say much but he thinks the world of Ma.

Sunday, 1st July

The rose card was from Alfred. He came round this morning (wearing Grandpa's coat) and we are friends again. We went to the Sunday market and strolled around arm in arm. I tied my hair back with the new kerchief Pa had brought for me and felt quite elegant. I wished we could bump into Emma but she'd probably still feeling bad with her tooth and wouldn't want to be seen with her jaw all swollen.

Alfred asked me about Jake and I told him the truth – that he's a sort of journalist and is writing about the strike and I am helping him with information. Not that I understand everything but I do work at Bryant & May's factory.

"So you're his informer," he said.

Informer? It sounded rather worrying and I hastily changed the subject, pointing out a flame thrower who had collected a small crowd.

"It's not real fire," Alfred assured me scornfully. "It's imitation. All a trick, like conjuring."

Imitation fire? I said nothing but I don't believe him. At that moment two hens escaped from a small wooden cage and Alfred and another man chased them while the owner, an old woman with a sack tied over her shoulders like a shawl, continued to scream for help. Alfred caught one of the chickens and returned it to the owner, who promptly broke its neck and sold it to her customer, for Sunday dinner. The other chicken was caught by a young urchin boy who then ran off with it, dodging and diving until he disappeared into the crowd.

"A nice free dinner!" said Alfred, grinning.

The old farmer's wife sidled up to Alfred and slipped a hen's egg into his hand by way of thanks. He was a little embarrassed but I said, "How kind of her – and how clever of you to catch it for her." He looked cheerful and quite different, and I made a note to myself to ask Ma not to call him Misery-Guts any more because it is rather unfair. I really do like him and maybe all he needs is a little encouragement to give him confidence.

I kept my eyes open for the little begging girl with the mug but we didn't see her. I uttered up a prayer for her. I hope she hasn't starved to death for the want of my ha'penny.

We found a shop that had a tray of stale pastries in the window.

"Only half price!" cried Alfred and he bought me a spice cake and he had a Chelsea bun, and we had a pleasant time of it.

Monday, 2nd July

The day started badly at home with Annie crying about her shoes, which she says are now too small and hurting her toes and making them bleed. Ma said she doesn't need to go to school but must help with the matchboxes all day until she gets some new shoes (meaning new second-hand shoes. New shoes would be a real luxury.)

When I got to work the day got worse. I had just stepped up to my bench when Sugden came along to say I was to see the manager. Not again, I thought, and my throat was at once dry. I could only nod and follow him, while all the girls shouted caustic comments or made rude gestures and piggy grunts – not to me but for the benefit of Sugden who muttered, "Bloomin' animals! I'd sack the lot of 'em!"

This time it was a different manager in a different room – I had seen neither before. He looked nice enough, with mouse-brown curly hair and a moustache. He had a stack of forms in front of him and I guessed at once what this interview was about.

He asked me if I could read and when I nodded he handed me one from the top of the stack and told me to read it. I should have said "No, I can't read."

My name had been written in the space provided. So this was the "declaration" the girls were being asked to sign. To give myself time to think, I read slowly, running my finger along each line as though I was struggling.

The form said that I worked for Bryant & May and found the factory a decent place in which to work. Well, I thought, it was not a bad place…

The form said that I was well paid for the work I do compared with other factories which manufactured quality matches. Was I well paid?

I glanced up and he was watching me closely so I

quickly returned to the form. It said that I considered the working conditions reasonable and that provisions were made for my well being. For example, the professional dental care offered, which when properly used would prevent the onset of jaw disease caused by a proximity to phosphorous...

"Well, Miss Finch?" He sounded impatient.

I just stared at him. All the other girls had refused to sign.

"Do you agree with what is written there?"

I shook my head, unable to speak. Struck dumb with anxiety, if truth be told.

"With what do you disagree?" His tone was weary. I suppose he knew I had been warned by the other girls.

I shrugged.

"You think you are badly treated?"

I decided to nod. That was a mistake.

He raised his eyebrows. "Can you give me an example, Miss Finch?"

I thought I had to say something and searched for an example. "Mr Sugden accused one girl of swearing but–"

"Was that you?"

"No."

"Please give me an example of ill-treatment to which you personally were subjected."

My mind, as usual, went a complete blank. I despised

myself for being such a coward. Pull yourself together, Florence! I told myself desperately but it did nothing to help me.

A few minutes later the manager handed me a pen and asked me to sign the form but I shook my head. Suddenly I recalled what Pa had said about strikes.

"One out, all out!" I told him in a quavery voice that seemed to come from someone else.

He sighed and took back the form. "I hope you don't live to regret this, Miss Finch," he said and pointed to the door.

I hope I don't!

Wednesday, 4th July

Pa sent me out as soon as I got home from work to find the old man who peddles second hand clothes and exchange Annie's shoes which are now too small for her. Pa gave me twopence to add to whatever the old man gave me in return for the shoes. His name is Joshua but he is known as Lanky Josh because of his long legs and hurried gait. We always deal with him and think him honest enough.

I found him striding along Dollett Lane with his sack

on his back and called to him to stop.

Turning, he snapped, "Now what is it, girl?" as though the very last thing he wanted was to stop walking and be forced to sell or buy something in the way of clothing. Lanky Josh has a gaunt face, a sharp nose and eyes like dark pebbles, and he smells of dust and decay. I always imagine him living in the crypt of a church! He would make a good wizard – or maybe a devil. That made me think of Grandpa's "pact with the devil" and I found myself smiling.

I held out the shoes and he instantly recognized them. "They've worn well," he said reluctantly. "Outgrown – is that it?"

I agreed. "Do you have some bigger shoes that will fit her?"

He set the sack on the pavement and crouched beside it, scrabbling through the contents with rapid fingers. He drew out a pair of small boots and I inspected them gravely. Scuffed brown leather, no laces, the sole beginning to part from the upper.

I shook my head. Another scrabble and this time he presented me with a pair of buttoned shoes, which had originally been a pale shade but had been stained red for some reason. I held the sole of one of them against the sole of Annie's shoe and saw that the red shoe was larger by nearly an inch. Three quarters maybe. The sole was also thinner. Were they suitable?

Lanky Josh said quickly, "Plenty of room there for the lassie's foot. A good shoe. Stuff the toes with paper. She'll grow into them in a month or two."

From him that was almost a speech. I think he found conversation tiring. We argued over the price but at last he allowed me a penny for the old ones and I gave him Pa's twopence. Within seconds he had gathered up his sack, swung it over his shoulder and was loping away, shouting "Old clo-o-othes!" at every sixth doorway.

Intrigued, I watched as a window was pushed up and a woman leaned out, dangling something that looked like a pair of stays. She and Lanky Josh were soon arguing on the doorstep until a compromise was reached and the stays and a few coins were exchanged. As he strode off again I wondered what it was like being him. Then I wondered what it was like being anybody but me. Then I gave up before I strained my brain!

But had I got a good bargain, I asked myself, hoping Pa would think I had. At least the shoes, being larger, would be more comfortable and we could cut out a piece of thick cardboard for each shoe while her feet grew into them. They might last another year, I thought, with luck and a decent winter, and I set off home.

My luck was in. Annie loved the colour, thought them "grown up" and declared the button strap "a bit of fashion!" Ma grumbled at once that they were "a sight too dainty" but Annie clamoured to keep them. She gave in reluctantly but added "Let's hope it don't rain heavy!" but Pa patted my shoulder which pleased me in a quiet way.

The church clock has just struck eleven and I am ready for bed. I shall now get down on my knees and make God a promise that if we go on strike and survive (meaning that we are not thrown out into the street to die of starvation), I will go straightway to the dentist at Bryant & May's and, if necessary, bear the pain of the drill without a word of complaint. I shall tell no one else. It will be between me and Him.

Thursday, 5th July

Ten o'clock at night. I'm tired out with excitement and anxiety.

A never to be forgotten day! It will be in all the papers. Jake turned up, as I knew he would as soon as he heard what had happened. I heard it all from Emma who had had her tooth removed and was back at work one floor above me. Seems it started in her department. We in our area, were getting on with our work, minding our own business and chatting with each other as usual. According to Emma later, two girls opposite her were told by their foreman to "Talk less and work more" or words to that effect. They had looked at each other and started to giggle. He told them to stop and to work in silence but they giggled even more, whispering to each other and winking at the other girls who were listening to what was happening.

The foreman was furious and shouted that if they didn't stop at once he would dismiss them.

Another girl shouted, "Don't take no notice of 'im! He hasn't got the guts to do it!"

One of the girls had called him "a bully boy" and before anyone knew what was happening, he shouted "Right! You asked for it! Get your things. You're going home!"

A sudden silence fell. Did he mean it? Was the girl sacked? One or two of the girls booed him.

"And keep your traps shut, the rest of you! I'm sick of all this insolence. As for you –" he stabbed a finger at her – "I'm reporting you to the manager. You'll as likely as not be fined for disobedience and you'll be lucky if you don't get sacked!"

For a moment everyone was frightened but then another girl rallied. Throwing down the matches she cried, "If she goes, I'll go!" And then other girls joined in and suddenly they were all throwing down their work and glaring at the foreman who was taken aback by what was happening. He had a rebellion on his hands, which he wasn't expecting and he didn't know how to deal with it.

I do wish I'd been there to see it all. Emma is so lucky. Anyway, the first we knew that anything was wrong was a clatter of footsteps and all the girls came rushing down the stairs, screaming for us to join them. I asked them where they were going, thinking it might be another drill.

"We're on strike!" cried one of them as they hurtled past us to burst out of the door with shrieks of excitement, into the sunlight outside.

It took us a moment to properly understand and then I thought "One out, all out" and I threw down the boxes I was packing and turned to Patty.

"Shall we?" I asked, though I already knew the answer.

She hesitated, glancing round, but slowly we all came to the same decision.

Patty shouted, "We're on strike!" and we all headed for the door to join our fellow workers. It felt very strange, as if we all shared the same mind, and that single mind had come to a decision. As Patty and I took to our heels the foreman from upstairs came rushing down and was joined by Mr Sugden, who looked as white as a sheet. I think they were probably as shocked as we were because it happened so suddenly and was entirely unplanned. The two foremen looked worried as they talked together in low voices.

Meanwhile hundreds more girls were appearing from

all corners of the building and when we finally managed to push our way out into the yard, I was astonished to see how many people were employed by Bryant & May.

I looked for Emma and saw her in a small group, heads close together, all talking at once. I was meaning to join them but Patty grabbed my arm and said we should stick with our lot. She looked less certain now, I thought, and I remembered that she has a baby to look after so maybe she was wishing this hadn't happened.

Suddenly a window opened up above and one of the managers put his head out and shouted, "Get back to work at once!" but he didn't sound very sure of himself and I expect he was as worried as we were.

Someone in the crowd yelled back at him, "We're on strike!" and a great roar went up from the women.

The manager shouted, "Stop this nonsense and get back inside!"

Another roar went up from the yard and there were hoots and jeers and catcalls, which embarrassed him so much, he drew back and shut the window.

Nobody knew what to do and we didn't know who was in charge but I supposed it was the two girls who had first walked out. Whoever they were. I wondered what Pa and Ma would say – and when Jake would appear like a bad fairy and start writing it all down.

A crowd was gathering outside the factory gates as word

went round that the factory yard was full of workers who seemed to be on strike. I felt a bit like an animal in a circus ring, with an audience coming to watch us perform. It was a dreadful feeling and I was beginning to feel slightly giddy, partly with excitement and partly with fear. Patty linked her arm through mine and, looking at her face, I saw that she was feeling uneasy too.

"What's going to happen now?" I asked.

She shook her head then added in a low voice, "Nothing good but we mustn't say anything. We don't want to draw attention to ourselves. They'll want to make an example of someone and I'd rather it wasn't me!"

"Or me!" I quickly added.

Then there was a crash as someone emptied out one of the dustbins and upended it. One of the girls climbed on to it and we all turned to listen. She said we should all go home now, in case the managers sent for the police, but we should all meet up again sometime and maybe go to Fleet Street to try to meet with Annie Besant and ask her advice on what to do next. Anyone who wanted to could go along but we should turn up outside the factory the next morning for further instructions.

The mention of the police had the desired effect and I and many others headed homeward. I was practising what I could say to Pa. My stomach was rumbling with anxiety and I was suddenly sweating and had to lean against some railings while I threw up my meagre breakfast. An old lady passed by as I did so and said I was disgusting, and she didn't know what the world was coming to. I felt like saying that I didn't know either, but I was too ill to care so said nothing.

My hand is cramped now from so much writing. I shall try to finish this tomorrow.

Friday, 6th July

It is now a quarter to eleven at night after a rather wretched day at home helping to make matchboxes. I feel nervous away from the other girls but Ma insists that I must make up the money by working at home. Once again Pa went out to the docks early this morning to see if he could get a day's work but without success. He wants to arrange a bare-knuckle fight in the hopes that he will win and thus bring in some money to last us through the strike. Ma says he is now too old and not even fit but he shouted her down and stormed out again, slamming the door behind him.

I feel terrible because I have caused this by joining the strike, but I am fearful of what will happen to me if I go back to the factory while the strike is on. I have heard of several girls who tried to return to work but were set upon by some of the strikers, which the police are calling "an ugly incident".

On Monday we are going to march to Fleet Street in the hope that we can talk to Annie Besant, who has an office in Bouverie Street.

The only bright note in the day is that Annie went off to school in her new shoes as good as gold. After a second inspection they are not as strong as they should be but it's too late now. Annie likes them so at least one of us is happy.

Monday, 9th July

When I arrived at the factory the gates had been padlocked which gave me an unpleasant feeling but I smiled cheerfully at the other girls. I suppose they were also hiding their true feelings. Jake was there, a pencil tucked behind his ear and a notebook sticking out of his pocket. He'd heard the news and was determined to come along when we went to Fleet Street, then write an article about us. He said we'd be famous. I replied that we'd probably be sacked. He said it would be a great triumph to be the first women to strike. I said it would be a disaster. He said we'd go down in history. "More likely end up in the workhouse!" I warned, but his mood was affecting me and I began to feel the beginnings of courage.

Jack told me, "I've made a banner for you, Florence." Leaning against the railings was a wooden handle with a square of cardboard nailed to it. On it, in red paint, were the words "Support the match girl's strike!"

I opened my mouth to refuse to carry it but Jake grinned.

"Say yes and I'll buy you some brandy balls."

He's really wicked, that young man. He knows how much I love brandy balls. I said I would carry the banner and he gave a great shout of joy and stabbed a fist into the air.

I must be mad, I thought, or stupid. Now, looking back, I can't believe we did it. I can't believe I was there, chanting about "fair deals" and suchlike, but I only carried Jake's banner for ten minutes because it was so heavy and awkward. Patty took it instead and by the end of it all she had huge blisters on her palms.

But it was exciting. We gathered in Fleet Street and chanted "Annie Besant!" over and over and crowds of people stopped to watch us and some clapped. One woman shouted "You tell 'em!" The police came and people started to boo them. They insisted we were hindering the flow of traffic which was foolish because London is famous for the traffic jams – the roads clogged with wagons, carts, brewers, drays, army wagons, commercial vehicles, horse buses, hearses, coal carts and farmers wagons. The list is endless.

At last Annie Besant got to hear about us in her office in Bouverie Street and sent someone down into the street to say that a few of the protesters could go to see her in her office. Jake pushed me forward, but I stepped quickly back knowing that if my name got into the papers Ma and Pa would be furious.

After our girls had their talk with Annie Besant they came back and said she was going to help us organize the strike.

They said that Miss Besant looked very serious and business-like. She had dark hair and wore a pale dress with stitching down the front and a round brooch on a dark collar. She was very kind and treated them like sensible people with a grievance and promised to do what she could to help us improve our wages.

Jake came back to Bow with me and the rest of the girls but then we went our separate ways, except that me and Jake stopped off at a stall for cups of tea and talked about it. I didn't tell him about Patty's blisters because I didn't want him rushing off to Patty to apologize and getting too friendly with her.

When I came back home Ma and Pa wanted to know all about it.

I said, "Annie Besant is going to highlight our cause – that's how she put it – and ask people to support us by giving money to a strike fund." They still looked very uneasy and without the other girls to spur me on, I felt that maybe we had bitten off more than we could chew.

Too late now, though. I was there and we did it. No going back.

Tuesday, 10th July

Last night after I'd put my diary away, Annie crept into my room and told me that Pa had a fight coming up on Thursday in a disused warehouse somewhere at the docks where the police would never think of looking.

"He'll be fighting a man called Johnny Wiseman who's nine years younger than Pa and a good fighter. If Pa wins he'll earn three pounds but if he loses he'll only earn one pound. But Pa will win. I know he will. But I'm not to tell you because you've got enough to worry about – being on strike and everything!"

I felt as though someone had elbowed me in the

stomach. Nine years younger! And Pa not well since he came home. I wish Annie hadn't told me but she has and it makes me feel it is my fault for being on strike. But it was Pa who had told me "One out, all out" I thought I was doing the right thing.

"Go back to bed," I told her. "I'll pretend I don't know."

I don't know what to think and I don't know what to do. Everything is happening so fast.

After Annie had gone I got up and knelt by the bed and asked God to make sure Pa won the fight because he has three children to support and if the other man is nine years younger, it's very probable that he has fewer mouths to feed.

I do wish I could find some way to help Pa.

Wednesday, 11th July

I dreamed about Grandpa last night, alive and well and laughing about something, and when I woke up it was so disappointing to know that we shall never see him again.

Jake turned up about six this evening – Ma says he is like a bad penny, only I do think she likes him and is sorry I am back with Alfred. She cannot complain, though, because he brought us a big dish of jellied eels and a loaf of bread so we had a good dinner together.

He says that some of the newspapers are taking the side of Bryant & May, which I think is a shame, but there are also more people joining in on our side. Charrington's has offered us the use of their hall in Mile End Road for a meeting, and something called the Trades Council is getting involved.

"Mr Bradlaugh is asking questions in Parliament about you girls," Jake told me, "and the way factory girls are treated – getting fined for misdemeanours and–"

"Mister who?" I asked.

"Not Mister Anybody. *Mis-demeanours*. That means small infringements of the rules." He was trying not to laugh at my mistake, which made feel an idiot and I had a sudden urge to wipe the smirk off his face – until I remembered Pa and the fight and realized that hitting people is hardly the right thing to do. (Unless, like Pa, you are trying to earn some money for your family.)

Jake talked for so long and so fast that I forget some of it but I do recall that the Match Girls have to be registered if they are to be given money from the strike fund, but we will hear more about that before long.

Poor Ma is feeling low, what with baby Dora being fretful and not eating, Pa going to fight again, and me being at home all day. She snapped at me saying, I was getting under her feet and the sooner I'm back at work the better for everyone.

I went round to see Emma for half an hour, worried because she had had her bad tooth out which was the wrong thing to do because it opens the gum. I shall add her to my prayers after what happened to Ellie, I don't feel very happy about it though I said nothing to alarm her.

Thursday, 12th July

It is now gone midnight and the candle stub is flickering so I'll be brief. I had decided to follow Pa when he went out to his fight but I told Ma I was going to meet Alfred so that she could not forbid me to go.

A thick yellow fog had chosen this night of all nights to settle over London and I dreaded the walk ahead. How would we find our way? I wrapped a scarf around my face to keep the foul-smelling fog out of my throat and nose. At the end of our road I managed to find Jake, who had agreed to come with me, in case Pa needed help. He had also covered the lower half of his face and joked that we looked like two conspirators! He had brought me an old floppy hat and I stuffed my hair up underneath it, hiding my face as much as possible and we soon realized we were following a stream of men who were headed towards the old warehouse, which was in a dingy, run-down part of the docks. The fog muffled the normal sounds, the street lights were of little use as we groped our way along, and the gas jets simply added to the already sooty fumes from London's thousands of chimneys.

My heart was hammering so much that I felt breathless and grateful that Jake was with me. He was finding it all very interesting and whispered that he might write about it sometime. Outside the rusty warehouse doors there were two hefty men acting as "lookouts".

"Keeping an eye out for the police?!" said Jake. He handed over a few coins, the entrance money, to the "gatekeeper" who gave me a funny look then said, "Not a good place for lassies!"

Jake had primed me. I replied, "My pa is one of the fighters."

He gave a lopsided grin, revealing rotten teeth. "Going to carry him home, are you?" The gatekeeper laughed. "You'd best stay at the back, out of sight, until it's over. It might get rough in there."

We pushed our way into to the dimly lit area and Jake found a couple of empty wooden crates for us to stand on. There was a sort of rough circle marked out on the ground with chalk and about fifty men of various shapes and sizes were gathered round, and money was being exchanged. I had not given a thought to the gambling side of it but Jake said it was illegal so that's why they needed to be warned if the police were going to raid the fight.

"Raid it?" I was becoming quite frightened. The whole business was darker than I had imagined – almost sinister in some ways – and I was glad that our position was in shadow so that we were hopefully scarcely visible in the gloom. From my vantage point I could see Pa stripping down to just his trousers, which he rolled up to the knees. His opponent was wearing knee breeches and both men had bare feet.

Everyone was either talking or smoking, or both, and the burning tobacco from the many clay pipes drifted upwards towards the rafters to form a cloud that hovered below the rusting roof. Jake bet sixpence on Pa and as the noise around us grew louder, I longed for it to be at an end before it had even started. Wiseman was shorter than Pa but stockier and looked healthy enough although his nose was distinctly crooked and there were fading yellow bruises on his upper arms – no doubt from his last fight.

I saw Jake placing his bet and asked Jake if he really thought Pa would win.

"No, but if I don't place a bet, it'll look odd."

Someone accidentally jabbed me in the back with what felt like an elbow, but although it pushed me forward I made no comment – afraid of drawing attention to myself and being discovered as a woman in a man's world.

Someone counted to three in a loud voice and the talking stopped for a moment while all eyes turned on the fighters to see who would land the first blow. I could hardly bear to look at Pa in case he should be knocked down within the first moments of the fight. However, the two men were dancing to and fro, circling round each other and making imitation lunges.

Jake leaned nearer and said, "Bobbing and weaving!"

I was too intent on Pa to answer and realized I was holding my breath. Suddenly Pa's right arm shot out and landed a punch on Wiseman's cheek, which made the crowd roar. The chatter began again as each man tried to interpret or anticipate the next blow. Wiseman retaliated then off they went again.

Jake whispered, "Ducking and diving!" and I sensed that he was trying to be humorous and I felt annoyed on Pa's behalf. I gave Jake the nearest thing I could manage to Ma's special "look". Pa says it would stop an elephant at 40 paces but Jake simply grinned and turned back to the fight.

When another blow landed on Pa's face his nose began to bleed and I wanted the fight stopped at once but no one else seemed to feel that way. Shouts of encouragement filled the air, which now seemed to crackle with a spiteful excitement – and then Pa hit Wiseman under the chin and

he fell back, tripped and went down to a chorus of boos.
I was so sure that the fight was over that I began to smile,
but within seconds the man was up on his feet again and
looking murderous. Now he was angry and the fight took
on a meaner style with flurries of blows, grunts and gasps,
which wound up the spectators to further shouts and
jeers.

I felt that Pa was flagging, but so was Wiseman and he
took another fall. This time he got up, hurled himself at Pa
and landed a blow under his chin. Pa reeled back, tottered
and fell. Jake took hold of my arm as cheers broke out
from the men who had bet on Wiseman, while the others
grumbled and muttered at the money they might have
wasted on Pa.

Instinctively I cried, "Oh Pa!" but fortunately no one
seemed to hear above the general racket.

"He's not finished yet, Florence. You'll see," Jack
reassured me.

I did not quite believe him but people in the crowd were
urging Pa to get up and get on with it – presumably the
ones who had wagered money on him. Pa lay where he fell
for what seemed like for ever but then slowly struggled into
a sitting position. He looked dazed and some of the blood
from his nose had dripped down on to his bare chest. I was
glad that Ma couldn't see him.

A man dabbed at his face with a wet cloth, wiping away

the blood, and handed him a bottle that Jake said would be water. Pa drank briefly, shook his head and ran his fingers through his hair to slick it back from his face. Then they were fighting again and it seemed to last a very long time, during which both men took several falls. Pa took most and was eventually floored yet again. This time he did not get up and the referee counted to ten and held up Wiseman's right arm, declaring him the winner.

It took forever before the crowd dispersed and Jake thought it safe enough for us to go to Pa and help him up. By the time we reached him, the referee had tipped a bucket of water over his head, which brought him to his senses but he was too weak to get up without our help.

Somehow we dressed him and, taking one arm each, began to guide him towards the door, but he didn't speak. His face was puffed and minor cuts oozed blood. He tried to walk but he was past it and we had to drag him all the way home, making slow progress through the fog. where Ma waited for him with a bowl of soapy water and a nip of brandy.

Afraid of embarrassing Ma and Pa, Jake made his excuses and left and Ma and I set about trying to revive Pa. When at last he opened his eyes he mumbled something we could not understand then pulled money from his trouser pocket and thrust it into Ma's hand.

"Thanks," she said in a gruff voice and there were

tears in her eyes as she stuffed the money into her apron pocket.

After we'd got Pa into bed she turned to me and said, "I'd rather end up in the workhouse than put him through that again." She leaned down and kissed him but he made no sound. She said, "Never again! Never, ever again!"

Friday, 13th July

An ominous date – the unlucky thirteenth! Spent all day making boxes and sticking on labels but wishing I was back at the factory.

Pa seems no better and we are worried. Ma made some broth, which he sipped, but he did not open his eyes and he has not spoken a word all day. I'm frightened and so is Ma, but we say very little and pretend that we can see more colour in his cheeks or that his breathing is stronger – trying to give each other hope. There is no money for a doctor, except the money from the fight and we think Pa would want that spent on the family – the reason for the fight in the first place. Also he has never trusted doctors and calls them "sawbones". They do have to saw off legs or arms sometimes but that is not their fault and many of the patients survive.

There is a rumour that the directors of Bryant & May are thinking of closing our factory and starting another in Sweden because they can buy timber for the match sticks more cheaply there. This would be a disaster for us and I hope they are just pretending to scare us into going back to work. But who knows?

Tomorrow we have to take our tickets to Mile End Road (to Charrington's Hall) to register and collect our strike pay. I wonder how they will decide how much we get paid. Whatever it is it will be better than nothing.

Saturday, 14th July

Nothing bad happened yesterday, thank the Lord, even though it was Friday, the thirteenth. Grandpa always said it was a foolish superstition (though he would never walk under a ladder!).

I thought Jake would be at the meeting but if he was I missed him.

When I arrived at Charrington's Hall there were not as many girls as I expected but Patty said a lot of them had gone down to Kent fruit picking. Some men were arranging chairs and the hall was divided into groups depending on where you worked at the factory so I sat next to Patty. There were boys there, too, who had been unable to work because we were on strike and I felt sorry that we had caused anybody else trouble but it all just seemed to happen.

Soon after eleven Patty cried "Here they come!" and three men came into the hall and they were carrying the strike money so everybody cheered. Annie Besant was with them and Herbert Burrows was there. We were told that they had collected a hundred and fifty pounds which is astonishing when you think how much that is.

Herbert Burrows explained how the money would be shared out. "If you earned more than six shillings while you were working, you will be entitled to five shillings. If you earned less than six, you will be given four. There will be five shillings for married women and widows…"

A young boy called out, "What about us lads, Mr Burrows? Don't we get nuffink?"

Mr Burrows nodded. "Certainly you do, lad. Boys will get four shillings and sixpence."

The boys cheered and threw their caps into the air and everyone laughed.

It was Annie Besant's turn next to speak to us and she told us not to go back to work until a proper settlement had been agreed. The London Trades Council was going to talk with Bryant & May. We had plenty of support, she said, and must not throw it all away. We all nodded earnestly and then someone called for three cheers for her and I thought we would raise the roof!

Then it was time to queue up for the money and, depending on which group we were in, we formed a line. We were all clutching our tickets and mine was 177 and I showed it to them and a man ticked my name in a register and counted out the money into my hand. I thanked him and was so grateful that my throat was tight when I thought how pleased Ma and Pa would be.

At least something good was happening, I thought, as I hurried home with a big smile on my face.

Sunday, 15th July

My smile did not last very long as Pa seems to be getting worse and not better. He still eats nothing and has not spoken although he does murmur and mumble as if he is trying to talk but cannot. Ma says bed rest will work the miracle and we must pray. At least Pa does not seem to be in pain and we are thankful for that. I hope Ma is right. I am trying not to hate the man who fought him but I do blame him. Surely he could have won the fight without hitting Pa so hard.

I haven't seen Jake since Thursday but Alfred came round to congratulate us about the strike fund and to ask about Pa's progress.

We went for a walk to the church to see Grandpa's grave and there had been another funeral with masses of flowers. Alfred said they would not miss a few and took some yellow daisies and put them on Grandpa's grave. It only has a wooden cross with his name on it and I felt sad that we couldn't afford a headstone and that he wasn't buried next to Grandma but I daresay they will find a way to be together in Heaven.

We sat down for a minute or two on one of the seats and Alfred told me that one of the newspapers had an article about the strike but said I might not want to hear it because it was taking sides with Bryant & May. I said I'd like to know what they said. He read bits of the article to me. I listened unhappily as he picked out the most important sentences and read them in a stumbling way which made it sound even worse.

'The strike of the match girls is still going on... It is not possible that this state of things can go on indefinitely. Their most ardent sympathizers will not be willing to continue to support them in voluntary or enforced idleness–'

"Idleness!" I cried indignantly. "Do they think we sit at home twiddling our thumbs?"

He said, "Don't blame me. I'm just reading it to you."

"I'm not blaming you, Alfred."

He asked if he should go on and I nodded.

"They must either return to their old work or must find new work of another kind … the end of a strike entered upon with inadequate resources and at the instigation of agitators … egged on to strike by irresponsible advisers–"

"Stop!" I told him. Infuriated I would not listen to any more and when he handed me the article I tore it at once into small pieces and scattered them over the path. Secretly I was hurt to realize that there were people who had little sympathy for us and were prepared to put their lack of sympathy into print for all to see. I told myself that Annie Besant was not an agitator, nor was she an irresponsible adviser. She was our champion … wasn't she? We had grievances which she understood. What did she have to gain by supporting us in our hour of need? Nothing.

"I daresay you'll go back to work sometime," said Alfred.

"Most certainly we will."

"When, do you think?"

"Who can say? Whenever our demands are met by the factory."

He had the sense not to ask anymore difficult questions and we were about to walk on when an elderly lady came along the path and stared at the scraps of the torn article.

She glared at us and asked if we were responsible for the mess. Alfred said no but I said, "Yes, but it's none of your business!"

She said I should be ashamed of myself for spoiling God's house. "Well I'm not ashamed!" I told her angrily. "I'm very upset and I'm sure He understands better than you do!"

Alfred blushed with embarrassment and grabbed my arm before I could say anything worse. When she'd gone we picked up the pieces and Albert stuffed them into his coat pocket and we walked on in thoughtful silence.

It rained hard in the evening and Annie got her red shoes wet and the colour ran on to her feet and she blamed me but I said she should have stayed in out of the rain. Ma is too worried about Pa to bother with such things, thank goodness.

Monday, 16th July

Kitty came round with some bad news that another of her neighbours who was a matchbox maker (working at home) had had no work since the strike started and so earned no money and was found dead at her table and her kitchen cupboard empty. "Not so much as a crust in the larder!" she told us, joining us round the table and reaching for a matchbox.

Ma said, "She won't be the last!" and shook her head.

"And did you hear about them girls what asked to stay at work?" Kitty demanded, her eyes wide. " They're saying some of the girls didn't want to go on strike but–"

"We all wanted to!" I said, shocked. "They're lying!"

Kitty shrugged. "I heard some of them didn't want to join the strike but was attacked in the street by some who did."

"Attacked? I don't believe it!" Everyone was looking at me as though it was my fault.

Ma said, "I wouldn't be surprised. Some of those girls are a bit on the rough side."

Kitty nodded. "A couple of girls turned up at the factory with black eyes! Mr Bryant was so worried that he asked the 'ome Office for help to protect the girls what wanted to carry on working."

"I don't believe it!" I insisted. I could not understand anyone not joining us when Annie Besant was trying so hard to help us. Surely, if someone like her thought we were in the right, everyone would see it her way.

Annie paused in her box-making to say, "If I was working I'd be in the strike."

Ma snapped, "Well you're not and you should be at

school." She didn't mean it because Annie is more use at home. Ma said to Kitty, "The new shoes don't stand up to wet weather. They're drying out," and glared at me. I pretended not to notice and dutifully dabbed the brush into the paste.

Kitty went on. "Seems the girls at some of the other factories are thinking of joining the strike and they're 'inting at proper picketing. You know – stopping people going in and out, with banners and whatnot."

(One of the other factories is at Stratford and it's also owned by Bryant & May.)

I did not know what to think

Kitty tossed another finished box on to the pile. "The 'ome Office –" she began.

Annie asked, "What is the 'ome Office?"

"The people what run the police. They promised Mr Byrant that –"

"And Mr May!" Annie prompted and got her ear clipped by Ma whose patience was almost exhausted.

"Ouch!"

"That's enough from you, Annie," cried Ma. Go and see to the baby," and Annie flounced off looking hard done by.

Kitty said, "The 'ome Office promised that if they do this picketing thing outside the Stratford factory, the police will be there to stop any fights."

I did not like the sound of this. I'd had enough of fights with Pa so poorly. I almost wished that Jake would appear because he made it all sound so exciting and now it just sounded dreadful. I thought of Kitty's neighbour starving to death and dying all alone at her table.

Now, as I write this, I cannot make up my mind about the strike. Will it be a good thing if it spreads to other factories or a bad thing? And did some of our girls really beat up some of the others? Ma thinks there are some rather tough girls who might but ... I don't think Annie Besant will be very pleased if she hears about it.

Tuesday, 17th July

Alfred came round this morning before work and asked to see Ma. She was in the bedroom with Pa, washing his face and hands, and trying to get him to say something – anything at all. When she came out, her eyes were red because she'd been crying.

"What d'you want, Alfred?" she asked wearily. "If it's about that dratted strike, I don't want to hear it!"

"It's not," he replied, rather taken aback. "I wanted to give you this." He thrust some money into her hands.

She stared from him to the money. "What's this about? I can't take your money."

"It's not mine, Mrs Finch," he said. "Not exactly. What I mean is, I did it for you. At the fight. I had a bet on the other chap – the one who won. I've taken out my stake money from my winnings and the rest is for you."

It was my turn to stare. "You were there? I didn't see you."

"I saw you – with that reporter chap."

Alfred made me feel terribly guilty so I thought I'd do the same to him. I said accusingly "You were there but you didn't bet on my Pa?"

"'Course not! I could see from the start who'd win – if you don't mind me saying. There was no way your Pa could beat Wiseman. I've seen him beat a man nearly twice his size!"

Then Ma burst into tears and to my surprise, Alfred put his arms round her. I watched speechlessly as he let her cry and I wished I had not been so unkind to him.

"That was very kind of you, Alfred. The money, I mean. Thank you," I said.

When he'd gone Ma counted the money and it came to seven shillings! She looked at it for a long time and then said we must spend a bit on a doctor because otherwise she thought Pa was going to die.

Wednesday, 18th July

The doctor came (the one from the end of the road who had looked after Ellie) and he looked very serious when he saw Pa.

"Is this the result of a beating?" he asked.

Ma hesitated. "It was a fight. He used to be a bare–knuckle man and we needed the money."

He stared down at Pa. "All those blows to the head – they do no good. The brain is easily damaged." He shrugged. "I suspect your husband will never fight again, Mrs Finch, and as to what else he can do…"

Ma said, "He's a deck hand on the *Tally Rose*."

"Was a deck hand!" He looked at Ma and then me. "I doubt if he'll ever be fit enough to go back to sea. That fight, if he lives, will have changed his life."

"Find another job," I said. "Is that what you mean?" I was feeling a great coldness as if all my body heat was drifting away and my legs felt like jelly. Has our life as we know it gone for ever, I wonder? Are we ruined – and all because of me? If I hadn't gone on strike Pa would never have thought about fighting again. If he dies, I thought, it would be me that killed him. Greatly agitated, I glanced at Ma to see if she was thinking the same thing but all her attention was on the doctor. Fearing that I might fall down in a faint, I sat down on a stool and took some deep breaths.

"But he'll still be alive. He can get better, can't he?" Ma asked. She explained that he seemed to hear nothing and failed to respond when we spoke to him.

The doctor leaned over him and lifted his eyelids to examine his eyes. Then he picked up Pa's hand and pinched the skin on the back of it. "Hmm. He doesn't react to pain. It looks like a bad concussion but there may be pressure on the brain, which would be more serious. It could lead to coma..."

He explained it to us. It seems Pa could go into a coma. The doctor says he had a patient once who was in a coma for 31 days, but the man was being fed through a tube. On the 32nd day he regained consciousness. "But Mr Bartholemew was a very rich man and was in one of the best hospitals in London."

"Bully for 'im!" Ma muttered,

"But don't despair, good lady. There is often a critical turning point. It's as if the patient is tossing up. 'Shall I live or shall I die?'" He closed his bag with a snap. "Your husband, Mrs Finch, is resting in the hands of the Lord!"

He is a bit pompous, our doctor, and he couldn't

save poor Ellie. But he means well … and he's all we can afford.

So now Ma is in a bit of a panic, not knowing what to expect and I'm trying to imagine how it would be without Pa or Grandpa. All the men in our family would have gone. I shivered.

Annie was at school, thank goodness, at least she needn't know what we are facing.

Kitty says a few sips of gin would probably work but Ma is afraid to try it in case she makes Pa worse. Certainly the doctor said nothing about gin!

When I close this diary I shall get down on my knees and ask God to forgive me. The strike was so exciting and being in the papers and meeting Jake … It was a big adventure, in a way, but today it seems like a bad idea because even if we win and go back to work with the concessions Annie Besant wants, nothing will ever be the same again for our family.

Thursday, 19th July

It's nearly midnight but there's a bright moon now so I am writing by the moonlight to save the candle. It rained earlier in the day and now Ma has decided that Annie's shoes just will not do. She sent me with them to find Lanky Josh but he was nowhere to be seen and a woman told me he had been set upon and robbed.

"Poor man!" I cried. "Is he all right?"

"Course 'e's not all right!" She gave me a withering look. "Two men went at him with staves and pushed him over so 'e's 'urt 'is knees pretty bad and lost a couple of teeth. Shook him up somefink terrible, they say. 'E's not a young man, is Lanky Josh. Forty if he's a day! And losing all his money and his sack of stuff! Ruined! That's what he is, poor old devil. How's he going to survive?"

Saddened for the poor man, I changed my plans and made my way to the pawnbroker, where our best clothes are still in hock, to see what shoes he had for sale.

I waited in a short queue – a man pawning his pocket watch and a young woman redeeming a threadbare blanket which hardly looked worth the threepence halfpenny she handed over.

Then it was my turn.

"Well?" The pawnbroker was about Pa's age but wizened with hunched shoulders. "Let's see it." His voice was always a bit hissy as though he might be ill with his lungs.

I produced the shoes and he tutted and shook his head. Ma had given me threepence from Alfred's winnings towards a new pair.

"Not worth a brass farthing!" he announced.

I was not going to let him get away with that and argued that they were little worn and still pretty enough.

He offered a penny and then twopence and I pushed him for twopence halfpenny but had to settle for twopence. He wrote in his ledger and gave me the money.

"Now I want some more shoes," I told him. "Same size. Plainer but stronger."

Pawnbrokers always have some things that have never been redeemed and can be sold on to a new customer. Children's clothes are quite often left unredeemed because the owners grow out of them before the parents can afford to buy them back.

Just then a large man came in behind me and pushed his way to the counter.

"I've come for our saucepans," he said. "Two of 'em. One with a dent. I've lost the ticket but we borrowed ninepence on the pans and we now owe a shilling…"

The cheek of him! I glared at him. "It's my turn! I'm being served!"

They both ignored me.

The pawnbroker asked his name and he said it was Fisher.

"Ah!" he shook his head. "Sorry, Mr Fisher, but you ran out of time a week ago. The date was on your ticket. Your fault, not mine. The pans are gone". He didn't look at all sorry.

Fisher thumped the counter with his fist. "My missus

says it's today, not last week."

The pawnbroker flicked back through the pages of the ledger. He ran his finger down one of the pages, found the entry then turned the book for the customer to read it.

Fisher shook his head. "Can't read, can I!"

Keen to be rid of him, I said crossly, "Let me see it." And saw that Fisher was, indeed, a week late with his money. When I told him he cursed under his breath and said, "She'll pay for this! Stupid whotsit!"

"Sold them two days ago." The pawnbroker sounded triumphant.

Fisher stormed out, muttering dire threats, and I felt sorry for his wife.

I finally found a better pair of shoes for Annie. Plain brown lace-ups, with one lace between them and slightly worn on the heels. Annie would hate them but Ma would call them serviceable and approve. I had to get it right this time. I paid the pawnbroker fourpence halfpenny and he threw in a long leather lace from a man's boot – one that we could cut in half so that at least Annie's laces would match. I knew I couldn't please everyone but I went home feeling slightly cheered.

Friday, 20th July

Annie is sulking about her shoes but I gave her a talking-to, pointing out that fussing over shoes was hardly nice while Pa was lying at death's door. She went off to school with a long face but returned in good spirits because she had made a new friend whose name is Elsie and whose mother makes fudge to sell in the market.

I walked with Annie through the market this evening in search of a bit of supper for the three of us and we found her friend's mother, who gave us each a square of chocolate fudge. We lingered in the market longer than usual partly, I confess, because we found it a more cheerful place than home, where Ma is worried and irritable and Pa is still not responding.

Kitty's friend says there are charities that help the poor to get into hospital but Ma is dead against the idea. For a start, she doesn't believe in hospitals because so many people go in but don't come out again. Also it's said that the hospitals sell some of the bodies of patients who die (for students to practise on!).

But if Pa doesn't come round by the end of the week,

Ma will send for the doctor again because the waiting is killing her. We are all waiting for the "turning point".

We had just bought some bloaters to go with our bread and butter when I saw the child again – the barefoot girl with the begging mug. She was standing at the roadside, staring into space, as dirty as ever. I dropped a penny into her mug but she seemed not to notice. She didn't thank me. I wondered if she even knew that she had any money in the mug. When I looked it was my penny and two halfpennies. I thought about how many there were in her family and how much they had to survive on.

"Shame, innit? Poor kiddie. No-one in the world!"

I turned to find a plump woman eyeing the child. She had a baby on one hip and was carrying a basket with a few root vegetables in it.

"No one?" I was startled.

"No one," she repeated. "'Er big brother died a few months back. 'E was the last one. They put little Lottie in the workhouse but she scarpered whenever she got the chance so they chucked her out. Pity, really. Poor little mite. She's gone a bit wild." She shrugged. "Doesn't speak no more. Lottie Godden, that's 'er name."

I stared at Lottie, ignoring Annie who was tugging at my sleeve. "Where does she live?" I asked.

"Just around. I've seen 'er once or twice sleeping in doorways. Once in the apothecary's and sometimes on the church steps." The woman's baby whimpered and she jiggled it impatiently. "Sometimes the police wake 'er and move 'er on but mostly they look the other way and leave 'er be. I doubt she'll last the next winter."

"You think she'll die?" I was horrified.

"Why not? She won't be the first nor the last to go that way. Die of cold in 'er sleep most likely. Be a mercy in a way." She sighed and moved on.

"Come on, Flo! I'm hungry and the bloaters are getting cold!" cried Annie.

I thrust the food into her hands and said, "You go on home and start eating. Don't wait for me."

When she'd gone I ran to the nearest pie man and bought a mutton pie. I took it back to the girl and handed it to her. She looked from the pie to me as though she didn't understand.

"Eat it!" I told her.

Cautiously, the child handed me the mug so that she could take the pie with both hands. All the time she kept her eyes on my face. She began to eat, nibbling at first as though she couldn't believe what she held in her hands. Then she bit more quickly biting into the thick crust and grabbed at the gravy that escaped and ran down the front of her ragged dress, trying to thrust it back into her mouth. I crouched beside her waiting for the last crumbs to be gone, intending to talk to her when she had finished.

Before I could open my mouth, however, she swallowed the last mouthful, snatched her mug and ran like the wind.

"Lottie!" I called. "Wait!" but she disappeared into the crowd. Puzzled, I tried to imagine what had been going on in her mind. Had she, perhaps, suspected that I might snatch her and carry her back to the workhouse? Had she assumed the gift of a pie was a trick of some kind? I stood up with a sigh and turned homeward. She hadn't uttered a single word.

Saturday, 21st July

This morning we match girls all went back to Charrington's Hall for a meeting and I saw Jake there with some other journalists. There was a man called the Reverend Stewart Headlam and there were people from the London Trades Council, who told us that they were going to have a meeting with Bryant & May in the evening to try and end the strike.

Then they said that they wanted a small committee of match girls to help the negotiations that evening. They wanted volunteers to form a strike committee. Plenty of hands went up and about a dozen were chosen. I didn't volunteer because I was already worried about the strike and, although Jake wanted me to, I refused.

I was sorry later when a photographer arrived and set up his camera to take a photograph of the Bryant & May Match Girls' Strike Committee. Annie Besant and Hubert Burrows and some of the strike committee stood behind the table on the stage and the rest of the girls stood below them on the floor of the hall. It was unexpected and the girls were all fussing with their hair, doing up buttons, rubbing at their shoes with the hems of their skirts and retying their neckchiefs. I lent mine to a girl called Sadie to hide her worn collar. Most of them would have come to the meeting in some better clothes, if they had known in advance that they would be photographed.

I've never had my photograph taken and it would have been fun though they were told not to smile but to look serious because of the circumstances. I think I look best when I'm smiling.

I won't be at the meeting tonight. I shall have to wait until tomorrow when Jake has promised to let me know what happened.

Sunday, 22nd July

Still no change in Pa. It feels as if we are living under a dark cloud and I keep wishing Grandpa was still alive. Although he was very old he was very wise and I'm certain he would have helped us in some way. Ma bought some meat bones and boiled them up and mashed in a potato to make a thin gruel, and we keep feeding it to Pa a spoonful at a time. Most of it dribbles down his chin but Ma likes to think some of it goes into his mouth and gives him some nourishment.

Jake came round to tell me about last night's meeting but he chose a bad time to come. Baby Dora was screaming her head off for some reason (griping in the guts, I expect) and when I gave her the last of the Godfrey's Cordial she spat it out all over me. She was red in the face with her eyes tightly closed and her small fists clenched. I put her over my shoulder but she screamed louder than ever. Ma lost patience and said, "Leave her be, Flossie. She'll cry herself to sleep." So I did, but Dora went on screaming until I felt like joining in!

Ma was busy getting ready to wash Pa – boiling some water and searching for what was left of our bit of soap.

She's gone quite mad on washing and washes Pa two or three times a day. I think it's because it's the only thing she can do for him. She can't talk to him because he doesn't answer, and she can't feed him properly. Poor Ma. She doesn't complain but her expression is grim and I know she is suffering under the strain. She has made up her mind he is going to die. Jake's visit was not exactly welcome.

Unaware that he was not very popular, Jake smiled at Ma and started his account of the events of the meeting. "Both sides stated their concerns..." (He sounded almost as pompous as the doctor!) "...and the London Trades Council listened to them but after nearly two hours the meeting ended and both sides were told to think over what they had discussed."

Ma sniffed, unimpressed. "Bit of a waste of time then, if you ask me! All sounds very grand and important but where's it leading? No where by the sound of it."

She sounded very irritable but Jake seemed not to notice. He went on. "But they have agreed to meet again next Tuesday to try and finalize things."

Ma tossed her head. "What a ruddy roundabout!" she snapped. "Words and more words! A bloomin' lot of hot air! Some people just love the sound of their own voices!"

She poured hot water from the kettle into the bowl, snatched up a flannel, the sliver of soap and a towel, and disappeared into the bedroom, muttering loudly about "bloomin' do-gooders lining their own pockets at the expense of the poor".

As soon as she had left the room Annie asked if she could go into the street to play hopscotch for a few minutes and I said yes though I knew Ma would disapprove. But Annie was suffering too, from Pa being at death's door, and she's only eight. I thought she deserved a break from the matchboxes.

I looked at Jake. "Do they get paid, those people – the London Trades Council? For sorting out the strike and everything?"

"I don't know," Jake admitted, after a moment's pause. "I've never thought about it."

I realized he would have to leave so I said I'd need to help with Pa's wash. Secretly I wanted Jake to stay so that I could have some cheerful company, but I know that was selfish of me. Jake finally took himself off.

Truth to tell, I'm now a bit tired of the strike and I do wonder what Queen Victoria thinks about it if she even knows about it. Probably wouldn't approve. I'm also worried about everything that's going on here at home. Pa hardly looks like Pa any more – very pale and his poor face puffy with bruises. His mouth was hanging open until Ma tied it in place with a strip of cotton torn from her petticoat. She is struggling to hold herself together. It's the not knowing. Will Pa suddenly die or will he come out of it and be like he used to be? And if he does come back to life, how can he earn his living if he cannot go to sea? He was only a sort of deckhand but it was regular work and the money was enough to survive on.

I just want to get back to work at the factory so I hope the strike committee sorts something out at tomorrow's meeting.

Monday, 23rd July

The church clock has just struck five in the morning. I woke up and cannot get back to sleep so I'm thinking about little Lottie Godden and wondering if she is awake and if so where she is. Perhaps I could make friends with her, take her back to the workhouse and ask the Master to give her another chance. Now that she knows how terrible it is to live on the streets she might behave herself better and stay in the workhouse. There at least she would be warm in the winter and would be fed regularly, and there would be other children in there she could play with – if they have toys. I don't know.

Thank the Lord the baby has been quieter today than yesterday. I went to the apothecary and bought some more

Cordial and gave her twice the dose because she seemed to be in pain. I think babies ought to learn to speak much earlier than they do because then they could tell us what is troubling them.

On the way out of the apothecary's I bumped into Emma who was going in with a prescription from her doctor. She looked thin and said she can't eat easily because of the pain in her jaw. She used to look pretty but now she doesn't.

Oh well! Another day. I must hide this diary and get up and count the matchboxes we made yesterday before the man comes round to collect them. He must have forgotten yesterday or else he was too busy.

It is now bed time and I am so weary. If only Grandpa had not died. If only we had not gone on strike and Pa hadn't been hurt. Why is it so hard to put things right?

Tuesday, 24th July

A day to celebrate. The strike is over and I for one am glad about it. We won! WE WON! Jake is as proud as punch that we will now have our own union and says it is a landmark victory, whatever that is. Our concessions have been granted! Three cheers for the newly formed Union of Women Matchmakers! Let me see if I can remember the concessions that Bryant& May have made:

1) There will be no more fines. We can blow our noses without being accused of wasting time at the bench!

2) If we have any complaints, we will now be allowed to go straight to the managers and not the foremen. That will, it is hoped, prevent some of the bad feeling that existed between workers and foremen.

3) Anyone who disobeys orders will be dismissed and so will anyone who destroys property belonging to the factory. (This is a new rule, not exactly a concession, but the Union has accepted it as fair.)

Oh yes! I nearly forgot.

4) Bryant & May will soon provide the workers with a room where we can eat our meals! Lordy! That will be something special – if it actually happens. Jake says it's easy to promise things. But then, if they don't give it to us, the Match girls' Union (or whatever we call it) will remind them and they will have to do it. Jake says we will be in a strong position.

I think there were other concessions but I've forgotten them.

Pa is still the same, which is a shame because we can't tell him the good news. Ma says he will soon be a bag of bones from not eating anything solid. She is so distracted by him that when she heard about the strike ending in our favour, all she said was "Thanks be for small mercies!" and hasn't mentioned it since.

Thursday, 26th July

Today I went back to work with all the others and it was quite an exciting time – everyone talking at once and all of us greatly relieved that none of us had been sacked. (In fact that was another concession we won – no sacking of the ringleaders (which we had feared).

We all worked very hard to show that we were grateful for the way everything has ended and bear no ill will. The foremen were polite to us and we were polite to them. (It felt a bit odd not to be taking the rise out of them because it used to be a bit of fun.) Still, they too were out of work because of us and must have been pleased to get back to normal.

Today I took a chance, secretly, on behalf of little Lottie Godden. In the lunch break I ran all the way to the workhouse and asked to see the Master but was told he was much too busy, so I spoke to a stern-faced woman called

Mrs Mackie who said she was his assistant. I asked her if they would give Lottie another chance, if I could persuade her to go back, but she at once refused. Rolling her eyes, she folded her arms which made her look even more fierce. "That girl is wilful and quite beyond control," she told me. "She upset the other children, stole from the kitchen and was rude to the staff. We don't want her sort here. She was a bad influence."

"But she's very young," I protested. "And all alone in the world. I thought the workhouse was meant to save children like her. She's quite desperate and–"

Mrs Mackie raised her hand to silence me. "It is meant to save biddable children," she said firmly. "Children who appreciate their good fortune. Not wild creatures like Lottie Godden who are certainly not biddable and are determined to cause trouble! Now I'm busy, Miss Finch. The answer is no. I must ask you to leave."

I thought briefly that I might insist on speaking to the Master himself, but in my heart I knew he would agree with her and enjoy doing so. I said, "How very un-Christian!" and walked away with my nose in the air. I wanted her to feel guilty but I don't think she was that sort of person.

So that is the end of my idea. I am bitterly disappointed that my grand rescue plan for Lottie has come to nothing. But I will not give up just yet. There must be something I can do for her.

Friday, 27th July

I got up early this morning and slipped out of the house. I went to the nearest church (the one where the Finch family are buried) and stood beside Grandpa's grave for a moment wondering if he would approve of what I was going to do. He would most likely grin and trot out one of his sayings. Probably "Nothing ventured, nothing gained!"

I said, "I'm not making a pact with the devil, Grandpa. Quite the opposite!" Did he hear me? Could he hear me? If only I had been able to give him one last hug before he died – but it had all happened so suddenly. My eyes filled with unexpected tears and I cried for a few moments, but then pulled myself together and wiped away the tears.

After a while I went back along the path to the church inside, which was greatly daring, for it was very gloomy inside, silent and quite empty. I have never been alone in a church and I found it exciting but rather frightening. It smelled of something sweet which might have been beeswax, and my footsteps echoed from every dark corner. High above, a flutter of wings startled me as a pigeon flew down from the vastness of the ceiling and swooped past me and out of the door.

Was God watching me, I wondered, as I tiptoed into one of the pews and knelt down. If so, he must surely know, all my sins. Did he approve of me and the girls going on strike? Had He noticed when Alfred stole the flowers from someone's grave and I did nothing to stop him?

"Dear Father God," I began in a whisper. "Please forgive me for all the bad things I've done, as I now want to do something good and I need your help..."

I stopped abruptly as I heard footsteps. I looked round and saw an elderly woman. She carried a basket full of cleaning cloths and had a broom resting over one shoulder, the way a soldier carries a rifle. Seeing me, she waved her hand airily and called, "Carry on, m'duck! Pay me no attention!"

She took off her shawl and got straight down to work, cleaning the brass eagle at the front of the altar and humming cheerfully to herself. It didn't sound like a hymn – more jaunty (like a popular ballad) – and I have to admit I was annoyed by her presence, which seemed rather disrespectful and threatened to spoil my sombre mood.

I lowered my voice, took a deep breath and started again. "Dear God, I hope you will forgive me for troubling you but there is someone you know..."

But did He know Lottie Godden, I wondered suddenly? Surely He should know everyone. But if He didn't...

The cleaning woman was coming closer so I glared at

her, to show my disapproval, I moved to the back of the church and knelt beside the font. It was made of stone and half full of water so I thought it could hardly need polishing. Closing my eyes, I gabbled my way through the words I had rehearsed, making my request and then my offer. I waited for a sign but none came though I still felt rather pleased with myself. I ran home, put the kettle on and let the day begin.

Saturday, 28th July

The match girls all met up at Charrington's Hall again today, to be given our strike money. Or should I say the last of our strike money because now there would be no more donations in support of our cause – it was over and we had won. People had been very generous and this time the total was more than 150 pounds so we were each given the same as last time plus an extra sixpence.

Annie Besant and Mr Burrows were there and a few others I recognized (but no sign of Jake), and there were short speeches, thanks and lots of cheers. Then we trooped out again and the rest of them stood around chatting excitedly because we had won a great victory and everyone said our strike would go down in history.

I, however, had more important things to do and I went straight to the marketplace in search of Lottie.

She was nowhere to be seen, I asked all the street sellers and the shoppers and no one had seen a child matching the description I gave.

"Kids like that are ten a penny!" said one woman.

A burly porter mumbled, "Dead, most likely, and tossed in the river!"

I did not want to imagine such a dreadful thing, but, growing desperate, I began to ask if anyone had heard of a little girl dying in the street.

A costermonger shook his head. "But if she's dead, then it's God's will. Best thing that could happen to her, see."

That made me think that perhaps God had taken pity on her and had ended her wretched life. It was a terrible thought. At last, however, a young woman suggested I ask at the church if a child had recently been buried. Why didn't I think of that, I thought to myself?

Back at the church I had to hunt for the vicar who was in his office room talking to another man about the evening service and which hymns they would sing. So I guessed he was the man who plays the organ – or tries to. When it was my turn I told the vicar my name and asked my question but he at once shook his head.

"A young pauper girl's funeral? No, Miss Finch. If the

child in question is in fact dead, her body has not been brought here for burial." He smiled kindly. "So there is still hope."

I went home feeling a little happier but puzzled as to what had happened to her.

Ma said Pa was much weaker and she thought the end was near. Annie had been crying and when I saw Pa I cried, too, because he was so still and reminded me of Grandpa. His eyes were shut and he looked dead but Ma said his heart was still beating.

I told Ma I was meeting Alfred later (which was a lie, so that I could go back and search again for Lottie). When no one was looking I buttered a thick slice of bread, folded it over and stuffed it into my pocket. So that made me a thief as well as a liar.

Baby Dora had finally stopped screaming and slept peacefully and we were all grateful for that.

When I went out again I searched the market place and was rewarded by the sight of Lottie. She was not in her usual place but sitting on an upturned crate beside a roadside cobbler who was tapping small nails into the soles of a pair of boots. A large woman hovered nearby, waiting in her bare feet for her boots to be finished. They must surely be her husband's boots, I thought, but then turned my attention to Lottie.

Her mug was on the ground next to her and as usual

she was staring into space. I approached slowly, afraid that she might run off but she turned her head and watched me without interest. I glanced into the mug and saw that it was empty. Crouching beside Lottie, I took the buttered bread from my pocket and saw her eyes widen at the sight of it.

"Listen to me, Lottie," I said firmly. "This bread and butter is for you and if you are here in the market tomorrow I will bring you another slice. Do you understand? You must come back here tomorrow and I will bring you some more bread and butter. Do you promise me you will come?"

What a foolish question. What did a child so young know about promises? How could she even think about tomorrow when getting through each day was almost more than she could expect.

But she nodded, eyeing the bread hungrily. I held it towards her and she grabbed it, stared at it a moment, then began to gobble it down, half choking in her eagerness and gasping for breath in between each mouthful.

The cobbler said, "You're wasting good food, lass. She'll not last much longer. Look at 'er ! A stiff wind would blow 'er away!"

Not if I have anything to do with it, I thought, remembering the pact I had made with God. Or tried to make. Who can tell?

I stood up. "I'll see you tomorrow, Lottie," I told her,

but she had finished the bread and now leaped to her feet, snatched up the empty mug and ran off into the crowd.

I glanced helplessly at the cobbler, who just shrugged then handed back the boots to their owner. The woman took them, admired them from all angles then sat on the ground and pulled them on. She stood up and dropped a few coins into his hand. "That's all I have," she told him.

Wagging his finger at her, he said. "So you still owe me a halfpenny!" he said, wagging his finger at her.

"Tomorrow for sure!" she told him unconvincingly, and hobbled noisily away in her clumsy footwear.

If only I could take Pa somewhere to be mended! If only he was a pair of boots, it would be so easy! Tap in a few nails, rub in a bit of polish and there you are. Good as new! As I walked away I told myself that even if I can't help Pa, I am doing the best I can for Lottie.

Monday, 30th July

Today I kept my promise to myself that if I survived the strike, I would go to the dentist at the factory. They were very pleased to see me and wrote my name down in their book. The dentist was a small man with dark hair. He wasn't handsome but he had very nice teeth. Well, he would, wouldn't he! (But then, he could hardly do his own teeth so he probably got another dentist to do them for him.)

At that time he and his lady assistant were full of smiles and I felt quite hopeful. After that, however, it was truly awful – tapping and poking at my teeth and then drilling the one that has the hole in it. Everything was clean and neat but it still hurt. In fact it hurt so much, I almost felt like jumping from the chair, running out of the room and taking my chances with the phossy jaw! Almost but not quite!

When it was done, the dentist beamed at me. "There. All done," he said proudly. "Your first filling! That didn't hurt, did it?"

"Yes it did! It hurt a lot!" I said, and gave him a really

nasty look. Poor little man. He looked so disappointed.

Still, I'm glad I didn't cry. I kept my spirits up by thinking about Pa and the pounding he took in the fight. He didn't cry or beg for mercy so I tried to be as brave as he was. Now it is over and I shall try and forget it. I might eat fewer brandy balls because they are sugary ... but I might not.

At least I won't die like my poor sister. When her teeth fell out and her mouth wouldn't close she never could look at herself in the mirror – and unkind people telling her it was her own fault didn't make her feel any better. I think, in a way, she was glad to die and that's so sad.

I wish I could tell Emma all about my filling, but it might not be a very tactful thing to do in the circumstances. I do hope she doesn't get phossy jaw, mostly for her sake but partly because she is my best friend and I don't want to lose her. But Ma, determined to look on the black side as always, says it doesn't bode well for her.

Tuesday, 31st July

When I came home from work Ma was missing and Annie was red-eyed and didn't look up when I walked in.

"Is it Pa?" I asked, terrified. My heart seemed to stop beating.

Two large tears trickled down Annie's pale face as she nodded. "Ma's gone to tell Kitty," she said.

I rushed into the bedroom on legs that felt like they were about to buckle under me. The sheet had been pulled up to cover his face. I took several deep breaths then carefully eased back the sheet so that I could look at him. He looked different. That was true. Somehow he had changed. But was he dead? I had seen Grandpa dead and I felt like a bit of an expert. I leaned closer, forcing down my panic, and studied him carefully. His skin looked almost transparent but some of the bruises were fading.

"You can't be dead, Pa!" I stammered, because that would mean … I reached out to touch his face but at that moment his eyelids flickered. Or did they?

"You imagined it!" I told myself in a whisper, afraid to hope.

I heard the front door close as Ma arrived back. "Kitty'll be round in twenty minutes," she said to Annie. Her voice was flat and dull.

One of Pa's fingers moved … or I thought it did.

Then Pa's chest rose and fell, gently, like a sigh.

"Ma!" I shouted, "Come quickly!"

Ma and Annie both rushed into the room as Pa's chest rose and fell again.

We all froze, watching what seemed like a miracle.

Ma was shaking her head in disbelief and the colour had drained from her face. "I thought he'd gone," she whispered, "and that's the truth!"

Annie and I watched as she bent over him and spoke his name. Pa murmured something.

Shocked, Annie turned to me. "Is he alive, Flo?"

I nodded. "It must have been the turning point!"

We hugged each other.

When Kitty turned up later, we told her the good news. Pa had come round. The doctor had said it could go either way and it had turned out well.

"It's bloomin' marvellous, that's what it is! It's a miracle," Kitty said, and went off willingly to fetch the doctor.

He came within minutes, delighted with the news, and told Ma what to feed Pa with to build up his strength. He also gave her a bottle of tonic free of charge, which was a wonderfully generous thing to do.

I said nothing about Lottie until much later when Kitty and the doctor had gone, the matchboxes had been collected and Pa had drunk some gruel and eaten a slice of bread, and was sleeping normally. Then I took Ma aside and explained.

Ma stared at me speechlessly. "You did what?"

"I just asked Him a favour," I explained. "I said a special

133

prayer that if He would take pity on us and save Pa, we'd take pity on Lottie. It was a … a sort of pact." Ma rolled her eyes and I rushed on. "An arrangement," I told her. "Like Grandpa said. I thought that it was fair."

Ma was looking at me as if I was quite mad. "Fair? How d'you mean? Your Pa was dying. This Lottie's not dying, is she? She should be in the workhouse. That's where she belongs."

"But she will die if nobody saves her … and she won't stay in the workhouse. I thought…" I hesitated.

"You thought what?" She stood with her hands on her hips which is never a good sign.

"I thought we could look after her a bit."

"Your trouble, Flo, is you think too much!" She tossed her head. "Always have done. I blame your Grandpa! Always filling your head with nonsense!"

I pressed on. "Spare her a bite of food. Give her a bit of a wash now and again…" I began to shake because I knew Ma was going to refuse. I decided I might as well go the whole hog. I took a deep breath. "I thought that maybe she … could live with us."

Ma's mouth fell open with shock. "Live with us? Live with us!"

"With you, Dora, me and Annie – and Pa!" I thought, "It's now or never!" and kept my eyes looking straight into hers.

Her eyes opened wide as it finally dawned on her and I almost saw thoughts rushing around inside her head. My last two words had spelled it out to her – Pa had somehow survived when she had thought him dead. There was a long silence.

At last she shrugged. "Take her a bite to eat then, if you must, and I'll think about it. But I'm not promising anything, mind. It's not something you can take on lightly … I don't know what your father will say." She tutted. "I don't mind giving her a bit of a wash now and then. Can't do any harm, I suppose…"

I tried to hug her but she pushed me away. That's just the way she is. Minutes later I made my escape with the bread and butter before she could change her mind.

Friday, 29th November 1889 (Sixteen months later)

Only three pages left in Grandpa's diary. I am saving up to buy another one. I think Grandpa would want me to carry on.

Today we went to poor Emma's funeral. By "we" I mean I took the day off work and took Lottie with me. She still

135

says very little and runs off from time to time, and Ma gets cross. Because I was taking the day off, Ma said, "Well, Flo, you can look after Lottie and give me a rest from her nonsense!"

Fair enough, I thought. It is my fault she is with us. She should be going to school but they find her troublesome. Annie takes her with her each morning – sometimes Lottie stays and other times she disappears which means that when I come home from work I have to set off again in search of her. She's not going to learn much at this rate though she's bright as a button. Maybe I shall have to teach her to read and write, the way Grandpa taught me.

I held her tightly by the hand now while she watched the burial through narrowed eyes. But she didn't shed a tear. She was the only one to be dry-eyed when baby Dora died nearly a year ago. I think, in a way, having Lottie here helped Ma to come to terms with losing the baby.

Lottie wears shoes now and today she had a warm shawl (which Kitty knitted for her) over her head and shoulders to keep out the chill November weather. When she is with us she sleeps on the landing next to my corner. It isn't perfect but she has a small straw mattress, a blanket, and a cushion for her pillow. It is better than the steps of the church or somebody's doorway.

It seemed only yesterday that we were all together at Grandpa's funeral but there we were in the churchyard again and Emma's mother was weeping and her father had his arm around her. Their lovely daughter has died from the wretched phossy jaw – probably one of the last people to die such a cruel death. It has been agreed by the match-making industry that in future matches will be made with red phosphorous (which isn't harmful) instead of the very dangerous stuff we used before.

Our Union of Women Matchmakers is very strong now and helps us in various ways. We have a clean room in the factory with tables and chairs where we can wash our hands and sit down and eat our food. After the dirt and dust of the factory floor, it's wonderful. If we have any problems or grievances, the union committee talks directly to the managers, and that's a good thing, too. (I may be on the committee next year – I am eighteen now and quite sensible.) The strike was exciting while it lasted and our conditions are better but I wouldn't want to go through another one!

Pa now works five days a week as a storeman for the small firm of Bestbury's – a local company which sells bricks, planks of wood and cement. He carries stuff around, sweeps up and sometimes works behind the counter, selling things to people who are building houses. He is half promised Saturday work as well – at a warehouse on the river in Limehouse, unloading barges – but it depends on the present man there being forced to give up from ill health. We shall see. The extra money would come in useful.

Pa grumbles that it is no match for being at sea, but since his illness, Ma is afraid to let him out of her sight! He earns a little less than he did on the *Tally Rose* which displeases him, but I keep reminding him that if he were dead (and he nearly was!), he'd be earning even less!

As poor Emma's coffin was lowered down into the grave I recall her dropping the violets on to Grandpa's coffin and how annoyed I was. Now it doesn't seem to matter at all. I shall miss her.

I am running out of space to write but I have saved the best until last. Alfred and I are walking out now and very happy together and Ma never calls him Misery-Guts. She wouldn't dare! I have met Alfred's widowed mother, who makes silk flowers for the hat industry. Alfred says she doesn't earn much but she prefers to be at home and couldn't face work in a factory. I think she approves of me. I liked her, anyway.

Oh yes! Jake is still around. I see him occasionally, rushing about, looking busy with his notebook, chasing the news. I saw him in the market once, with a pretty young lady who was clutching his arm. I wouldn't change Alfred for the world – but I shan't forget Jake. (I shall always have happy memories of the pie and mash with gravy!)

All in all, life is good…

HISTORICAL NOTE

When the match girls went on strike in 1888 Queen Victoria had been on the English throne for 50 years and the British Empire appeared to be still flourishing. Prince Albert (the queen's husband) had died in 1861 and Queen Victoria had retreated into a prolonged state of mourning ,which caused resentment among her people, who were seldom offered a glimpse of their monarch.

The Great Exhibition in Hyde Park in 1851 (inspired by Prince Albert) had been a huge success. It brought thousands of foreigners to England to marvel at its wonders but too many desperate Londoners were unable to attend, needing every shilling they could earn to keep body and soul together, and unwilling to spend on such frivolities while the shadow of the workhouse threatened the impoverished.

The main reason for the increase in both wealth and poverty was the industrial revolution. The creation of engine power instead of horsepower meant that mass production could begin and this meant factories, which sprang up throughout London and other cities. This brought financial success to factory owners as well as to rich men who invested their money, by way of shares, in the companies. However, the change from horsepower to engines put an end to many of the jobs that had once existed in the countryside. Out-of-work farmhands, farriers, blacksmiths and the like needed to move to cities in search of a totally different kind of employment. This was made easier by the railways which hurried them to and fro. Unfortunately, many of them decided to live in London, where the housing stock was totally inadequate because many streets had been pulled down to make room for the expanding railways. This meant increased overcrowding and led to dangerously insanitary conditions.

London was on the way to becoming the largest city in the world, with all the problems that produced, and the population eventually found itself divided by wealth, or the lack of it.

The so-called "gentry", safe in their big houses and surrounded by servants, set out in their carriages to enjoy the social delights that London offered them. They picnicked in their small boats on the Thames at the Henley Regatta, or watched Oxford and Cambridge rowing teams race at Putney; they enjoyed shooting parties on their country estates; they donned their fine clothes and attended the opera at Covent Garden or plays at the many theatres scattered throughout London's West End. In 1887 they no doubt gave private dinner parties, to celebrate Queen Victoria's 60 years on England's throne.

They tried to ignore the risks posed to them by the

thousands of poverty-stricken inhabitants who lived among them in the many pockets of deprivation in and around London. Thousands of people were trying to survive in terrible conditions, many slowly starving, all prone to the ravages of cholera, typhoid, tuberculosis, diphtheria, smallpox and other diseases that were spread by overcrowding and insanitary conditions – no fresh water and no mains drainage. Mostly self-employed as costermongers or stallholders, or doing casual work in the docks or on construction sites, many others were without any paid employment at all and scratched a living from the rubbish tips or from what they could scavenge along the banks of the Thames when the tide was out.

The so-called middle classes were somewhere between the rich and poor, holding down regular office jobs as clerks, railway employees, teachers, doctors and many other "nine-to-five" workers who went home each evening to their well-built houses, mostly on the outskirts of the city, deeply thankful for regular employment and a secure roof over their heads.

It was almost inevitable that the poor, many of them helpless, jobless and homeless, began to turn their frustration on the government. When this turned to anger, the authorities (haunted by the memories of the French Revolution) were seized by a suspicion that a revolution might be developing in Britain.

Crime was a growing problem but while the much-praised, recently formed Metropolitan Police Force was claiming success, murder by way of stabbings, shootings, poisoning and the like, still earned the ultimate punishment – hanging. Lesser crimes resulted in imprisonment and finally a new modern prison known as Pentonville was built in 1842. In 1888 the police force was severely challenged by the infamous "Jack the Ripper" who murdered women in Whitechapel but was never caught.

More insidious, perhaps, was a new form of social disorder which began to appear. This was strike action, taken by disgruntled workers who chose to withhold their labour to draw attention to their grievances. The complaints included poor working conditions and low wages. The seamen were unhappy, the dock workers dissatisfied, the coal miners began to agitate and so did the engineers. By the end of the nineteenth century all had taken strike action – and so, of course, had the Bryant & May match girls!

Beyond Britain's borders we were engaged in two major conflicts – the Crimean War and the Indian Mutiny and thousands of young men enlisted in the army. Fighting in battle was a dangerous occupation but the pay was sufficient and the army rations were reasonably regular. Nobody knew that, as the century drew to a close in 1899, we would again be at war – with the Boers in South Africa.

On the bright side, Britain had much to be proud of during the nineteenth century. We had become a great trading nation and the Port of London saw imports from all over the world, brought in by fast sailing clippers, and our newly manufactured goods were sent out in the same way to far-off lands.

Exploration continued in Africa, where the Scottish explorer Dr David Livingstone tracked the source of the River Nile.

Medical advances were being made – in 1853 an Act was passed to make vaccination against smallpox compulsory and in the same year the queen was given chloroform during the birth of her child. The English surgeon Joseph Lister discovered antiseptics, a stethoscope was invented and microscopes were greatly improved.

The English engineer Isambard Kingdom Brunel designed many of Britain's wonderful bridges and introduced us to his new steamships.

As the nineteenth century drew to a close and the church bells rang in the new year, no one knew what the twentieth century would bring. Change, however, was not long in coming. On 22 January 1901 Queen Victoria died, aged eighty-one. Her son Edward took the throne and the "Edwardian era" was ushered in.

TIMELINE

1834 Poor Law Unions create workhouses for the destitute, supervised by local Masters.

1837 William IV dies. Princess Victoria becomes queen.

1842 Pentonville Prison is built in Holloway – modern and humane.

1844 Famine in Ireland causes emigration to the United States.

1851 The Great Exhibition is held at Crystal Palace in Hyde Park, London.

1853 Medical advances are made, including the compulsory vaccination against smallpox and the use of chloroform used during a royal birth.

1853-56 The Crimean War (Florence Nightingale's improved nursing regime improves military hospitals).

1859 Work starts on the Victoria and Albert Museum.

1865 The American Civil War ends. President Abraham Lincoln is shot.

1888 Great social unrest. Bryant & May match girls strike and win, and later form the Union of Women Match Makers.

1897 Queen Victoria's Diamond Jubilee, celebrating her 60 years on the throne.

1889-1901 The Boer War.

1901 Queen Victoria dies. Her son Edward becomes king.

Experience history first-hand with My Story –
a series of vividly imagined accounts of life in the past.

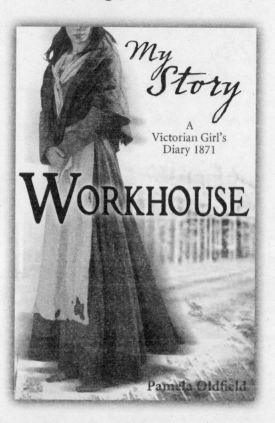

It's January 1871 when Edith, the sheltered
daughter of a wealthy widow, pays her first
eventful visit to the workhouse for the poor. There she
meets Rosie, a rebellious, quick-tempered orphan
who is always getting into trouble. Edith soon finds
herself drawn into Rosie's wild schemes and
both their lives are never the same again...

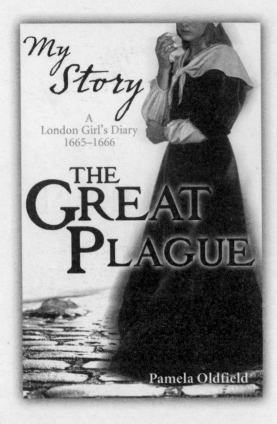

My Story

A
London Girl's Diary
1665–1666

THE
GREAT
PLAGUE

Pamela Oldfield

It's 1665 and Alice is looking forward to being
back in London. But the plague
is spreading quickly, and as each day passes
more red crosses appear on doors.
When her aunt is struck down with the plague,
she is forced to make a decision
that could change her life forever...

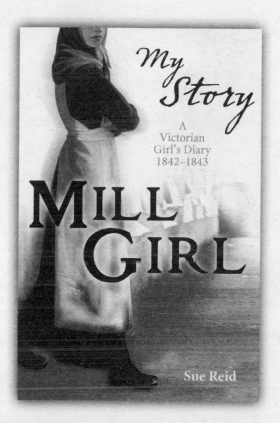

My *Story*

A
Victorian
Girl's Diary
1842–1843

MILL
GIRL

Sue Reid

In spring 1842 Eliza is shocked when
she is sent to work in the Manchester cotton
mills – the noisy, suffocating mills. The work is
backbreaking and dangerous – and when she sees her
friends' lives wrecked by poverty, sickness
and unrest, Eliza realizes she must fight to escape
the fate of a mill girl...

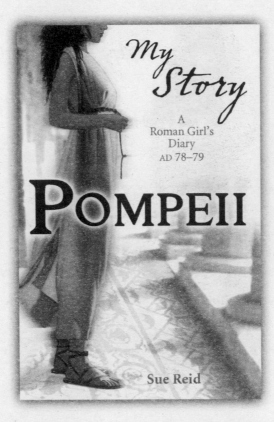

My Story

A
Roman Girl's
Diary
AD 78–79

POMPEII

Sue Reid

It's August AD 78 and Claudia is at
the Forum in Pompeii. It's a day of
strange encounters and even odder portents.
When the ground shakes Claudia is
convinced it is a bad omen. What does it all mean?
And why is she so disturbed by Vesuvius,
the great volcano that looms over the city...

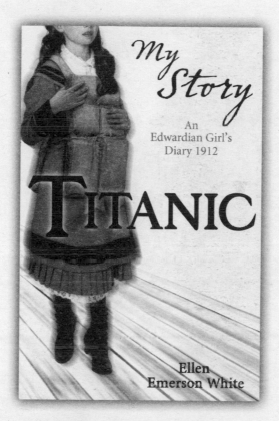

My Story

Story

An
Edwardian Girl's
Diary 1912

TITANIC

Ellen
Emerson White

Margaret Anne dreams of leaving
the orphanage behind, and she can hardly
believe her luck when she is chosen to accompany
wealthy Mrs Carstairs aboard the great Titanic.

But when the passengers are woken on a
freezing night in April 1912, she finds herself
caught up in an unimaginable nightmare...

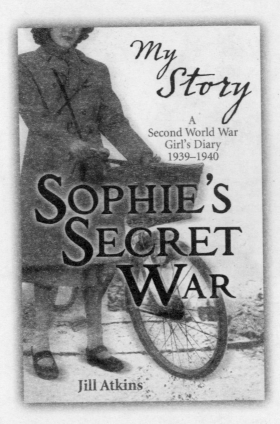

In 1939, the start of the Second World War,
Sophie becomes a messenger for a Resistance
group in Northern France. But as the
German invaders overwhelm the British forces
on the French coast, Sophie finds herself more
deeply involved with the Resistance – in a
dangerous plan to save a young Scottish soldier...

My
Story

An
Irish Girl's Diary
1845–1847

THE
HUNGER

Carol Drinkwater

It's 1845 and blight has destroyed the precious
potato crop leaving Ireland starving.
Phyllis works hard to support her struggling family,
but when her mother's health deteriorates
she sets off in search of her rebel brother
and is soon swept up in the fight for
a free and fair Ireland...

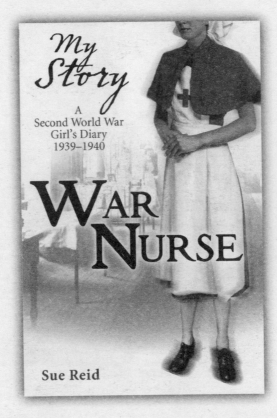

My Story

A
Second World War
Girl's Diary
1939–1940

WAR NURSE

Sue Reid

When **war breaks** out in **1939 Kitty** signs up
to be a **Red Cross nurse** in a **military hospital.**
And it's not long before she's treating **badly**
wounded casualties from the war now **raging**
across **Europe.** Then the hospital takes a
direct hit and Kitty finds herself
a **reluctant heroine...**

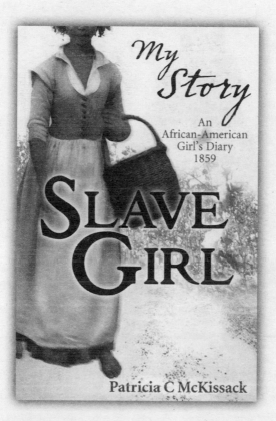

My Story

An
African-American
Girl's Diary
1859

SLAVE
GIRL

Patricia C McKissack

In 1859 it's illegal for slaves to read and write,
but Clotee is teaching herself in secret.
"Freedom" is just another word she's learned to write.
Then she finds out about the Underground Railroad, a
network of people who help runaway slaves, and
discovers that freedom is more than just a word...

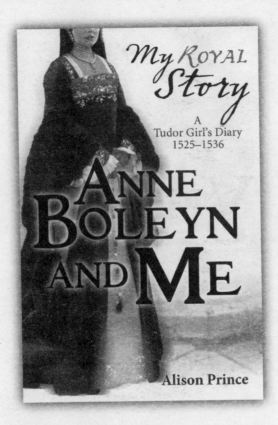

My ROYAL
Story

A
Tudor Girl's Diary
1525–1536

ANNE
BOLEYN
AND ME

Alison Prince

It's 1525. **Elinor** is lady-in-waiting to
Queen Catherine. **Anne Boleyn** is also one of the
Queen's ladies until she attracts the eye of
King Henry. Elinor watches and listens,
and writes down all she sees in her journal –
a witness to **Henry's** desire for a son that
tore his family and his kingdom apart...

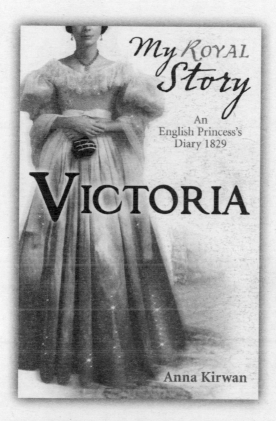

My ROYAL *Story*

An
English Princess's
Diary 1829

VICTORIA

Anna Kirwan

In 1829 Victoria is a lonely little girl, being
brought up in obscurity by her widowed mother.
But Victoria is no ordinary child.
King George IV is her uncle, and she is the
eldest grandchild of King George III. She is closer
to the throne than she ever imagined. Someday she
will be Queen Victoria...

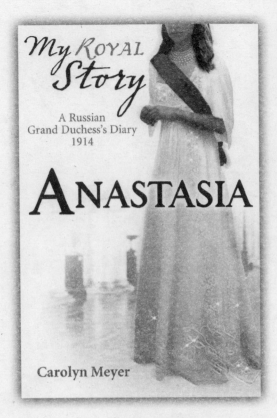

My ROYAL Story

A Russian
Grand Duchess's Diary
1914

ANASTASIA

Carolyn Meyer

In 1914 Grand Duchess Anastasia, youngest daughter of the Tsar, leads a regimented but privileged life in the grand palaces of Russia. Then come the First World War and the Bolshevik revolution. With the royal family arrested and exiled to Siberia, the life she knew is swept away forever. Fear and uncertainty are all that remains...